MW00889691

# KHAN:
# A MAINE COON

Semi-fictional Biography

Written & illustrated by

## Marie J. S. Phillips

# KHAN: A MAINE COON

© 2003 by Marie J. S. Phillips.

Library of Congress:  TXu 1-088-338

First Edition: ©2011 by Marie J. S. Phillips & LuLu .com,

ISBN:978-1-4583-2466-5

## **DEDICATIONS**

To my wonderful husband, Ed Phillips, whose love and support over the decades proved priceless, because without such,  all in my life, including the real cats who inspired this book, would not have been possible.


To my friend and mentor, Mr. David Ayscue, (November 1953 - September 2010) who proof read my work, and taught me proper punctuation techniques, bequeathing to me an invaluable gift I shall treasure for the rest of my writing life.

## IN LOVING MEMORY

To my Mom, (January 31, 1931 - May 16, 2006), who always encouraged me to get an education, and follow my heart.

To all my past beloved feline furbabies, who made this book possible: Khan (May 10, 1991- April 10, 2002), Phantom (July 22, 1991 - Aug 7, 2007), Mandee (May12, 1987 - March 26,1999), Indy (July 4, 1993 - Jan 9, 2008) Munchkin (1992? - Oct 31, 2000), Demon (April 1990 - August 6, 1991) Black Satin (? - January 2008)

## CHAPTER 1: HIS MAMA

Tiger watched the stranger carry his littermate out of the house. He twitched his long tail with fear and curiosity, then turned his head to face his mother, a beautiful classic red tabby Maine Coon cat.

"Mama? Why are they taking Patches away?"

"The stranger will be Patches' new human momma, like my momma is to me," his mother, Duchess, purred in answer. "Don't fret, my little one. You are so big, strong, and handsome. Someone will see this, and take you to your new life."

Little Tiger gazed into his mother's copper eyes, then snuggled against his remaining siblings to nurse. Over the next few days, his mother's milk trickled slowly, then stopped whenever Tiger suckled for more than a few moments. His siblings left his mother's side,

5

but Tiger sucked harder, until Duchess pushed him away with a paw. He protested with a mew.

"You must eat real food now. You are almost two full mooncycles old, and no longer need my milk," she said sternly, slanting back her tufted ears. She flicked her tail. "There is your food. I have no more milk. You must eat it to keep growing strong."

Tiger turned, peeking over the edge of the kittening box, and spied a bowl of mush. He leaped out of the box, toddled over, sniffed, then licked the mixture. He wrinkled his face in disdain, but his little sister dove into the shallow metal bowl, lapping up the mush with gusto. He sat down. Duchess rose to her feet, and joined him at the big bowl. She lapped up a few mouthfuls, then turned to Tiger.

"If you don't eat, I will drag you by your scruff, and dunk your nose in it."

The kitten mewed protest, but obeyed his mother. He lapped up the mush, and, after a few gulps, decided it tasted very good. His stomach growled, and he plunged his face into the food, eating heartily. He jostled his littermate, and his sister squalled protest.

"Mama! Tiger stepped on me!"

"I did not!" Tiger lifted his head from the bowl. Food dripped from his chin onto the beige linoleum floor. He glanced at his sister. Baleful green eyes glared at him from her orange, black, and white face. Callie's fuzzy coat bristled her outrage.

"Come on, Callie. Don't be such a baby. Eat with me," Tiger mewled to her. Callie sat up, shook her tousled calico coat, and rushed back to the bowl. She squeezed between him and her black-and-white brother, who cuffed her with a strong white paw.

"Callie, you're a hog."

"You never saw a hog so how do you know I am one?" Callie retorted.

"Mama told me," Tux insisted. She ignored Tux, and dove into the food.

"Mama said hogs are pigs, and they are big animals that like to eat anything," Tiger added, then lapped up food. Behind Tiger, his mother lay back down, and purred approval.

Days passed. One morning broke hot and humid. Tiger drank water, and greedily ate his breakfast. He ran to his mother and tried to nurse, but found no milk flowing. He mewled his disappointment.

"What a baby you are," Tux said, smacking him with a white paw. "Mama has no more milk. Hasn't for days and days."

"So? I can try, can't I?" Tiger hissed, and jumped on his brother. They wrestled in glee, careening around the kittening box, tumbling out onto the wooden floor. They chased each other around the room, then finally collapsed beside their mother. She groomed both frazzled kittens, and Tiger purred, enjoying the relaxation.

The doorbell chimed suddenly, interrupting the quiet morning. The two family dogs erupted into full ruckus. As the big gentle German Shepherd barked, and his tiny Pomeranian companion yapped shrilly, a woman walked into the room where the nest lay.

Duchess uttered a low growl, eyeing the two dogs, who wagged their tails but dared not enter the room. Duchess resumed purring as the stranger cooed over Tiger's siblings, and patted Tiger's head.

"This calico and the tuxedo are beautiful. That poor tabby, however, is quite cow-hocked. He may even have problems with his hips." The woman picked up Callie and Tux. "I will take both."

"Mama! Tiger! I'm scared!" Callie mewled her fright. Tux merely purred, hanging limp in the woman's grasp.

"Do not fear, my baby Callie," Duchess purred soothingly. "This will be your new momma. Do not fear."

"Poor little one," the woman crooned to Callie. "I will love you. Don't fear."

Callie quieted down, then the soft-spoken woman whisked her and her brother away. Tux called out once.

"Hope you get a good home, too, Tiger!"

Tiger gazed at his mother as the dogs quieted down.

"I have a good home." Tiger flicked his tall ears. "What is cow hocks?"

"I am not sure, little one," Duchess answered, sadness in her tone. "But I believe it has something to do with your back legs."

"I feel fine." Tiger tilted his head.

"I know," Duchess licked his ears. "Do not worry about it. Eat, and be strong. You are so big now. My big boy."

Tiger ate his meal, finishing every speck, which had changed in texture over the last few days from mostly milk to a more strong-smelling mushed meat. Time passed, and no more strangers arrived to see Tiger. His mother groomed him with pride, and Tiger thought perhaps he might stay with his mother. One morning, Duchess groomed him, pride in every stroke of her rough tongue.

"You are so big!" Duchess purred to him. "I think you will be like Big Mike, your sire. What a handsome Tom he is."

Tiger enjoyed his life, trying not to dwell on what the visitor said about his legs. One evening, the neighbor woman arrived, bringing a huge brown tabby on a leash. Duchess eagerly greeted the gentle male Maine Coon.

"Tiger! This is your sire. Oh, so big and handsome!" she purred, rubbing her body along his. Tiger watched Big Mike with awe, then approached, his tail rising above his back, curving over like a giant furry candy cane. He sniffed the tom's nose.

"Fine boy," Big Mike purred, and sniffed Tiger's nose. "I am surprised he is here. You are keeping him?"

"I hope so." Duchess twitched her tail. "Nobody has come to take him away. My momma may let him stay with us."

"Play?" Tiger asked.

Big Mike's face broke into a feline smile, eyes closed, whiskers forward as he blinked.

"Yes!" The Maine Coon tom romped with Tiger, gentle and careful. Tiger chased his father's tail, jumped on his back, wrestling him in delight. The dogs joined in, respectful of Big Mike's huge-clawed paws. The children laughed, and Tiger thought this a most wonderful day. Finally, Big Mike sat down beside Duchess. The dogs lay down, panting, and the children left for other interests.

"Rest, young one," he purred. "I am tired."

Tiger snuggled between both his parents. He fell asleep, delighted with life, but dreamed unsettling images of misshapen hips and back legs.

© Marie J.S. Phillips

## CHAPTER 2: THE SHELTER

"Noooo!" The sudden yowl from his mother jerked Tiger awake.

"Mama?"

"Noooo!" Duchess protested again as her human momma picked up Tiger. Tiger flattened his ears, and mewled, a sad cry that sounded like "meh!" He saw daylight streaming in the windows, and realized he slept through the entire night, exhausted by the wonderful play with his father.

"Nooo!" his mother wailed again, shattering Tiger's memories of the day before.

"I am sorry, Duchy, I am, but nobody wants him. We can't keep him, so I am taking him to a shelter where someone can adopt him."

"Nooooo!" Duchess yowled as the woman pushed Tiger into a carrier.

"Mama!" Tiger mewled, sensing his mother's distress.

"Poor Duchess. I have no choice. This will be your last litter, too. You'll be spayed so you can't have any more kittens. It is getting too hard to sell your kittens; because neither you nor Big Mike have papers, I can't prove your babies are purebred. To get your pedigree, I'd have had to spay you before your first litter. That's what the breeder contract says about pet-quality kittens. But I wanted you to have babies anyway. Same with Big Mike, except he'd have been neutered so he could not breed either. I wish I could make you understand." The woman patted Duchess' head, then walked toward the door. Duchess leaped up and ranged in front of the woman.

"Noooo!" Duchess wailed. "I don't care about stupid papers! If he is my last baby, don't take him away!"

"Duchess, behave now," the woman scolded. "We can't keep him any longer. He is so big -- he already looks almost grown."

His distraught mother rubbed against the door of the carrier, her red fur filling his vision through the crate's bars. His ears quivered with her distressed wailing as the woman carried him out of the home he loved.

"Mama!" he cried, his mew coming out soft, low, and lamblike. The woman opened the door of a strange blue contraption. Tiger peered at the car, mystified and scared. The woman set his carrier down inside the vehicle. Soon, he bounced and gyrated as his world suddenly moved. He curled up against the rear of the crate -- calm outside, scared inside. The carrier finally stopped vibrating, and all went quiet. Tiger's owner lifted him, swinging the box around. Dizzying sights met his blinking amber eyes. He heard dogs barking, and, as the woman carried him closer to the huge building, cat voices floated to his ears. Tiger listened, twitching his ears at the uncertain voices. The woman brought him into the shelter, setting the carrier on a counter.

"Can I help you?" a stranger's voice asked.

"Yes. I am sorry, but we can't keep this kitten. I can't even give him away," she said.

"Why not?" The young woman behind the counter frowned. Tiger sensed her disapproval.

"We have too many mouths to feed as it is."

"You do know we aren't a no-kill shelter," the shelter worker warned. "There *are* others in Connecticut that are no-kill."

"Yes, I know, but you're the closest to my home. I just can't keep him. He's a kitten. Someone should take him. Just find him a home, OK?"

"Sure. How old is he?" the shelter worker's voice lowered with obvious annoyance. Tiger trembled, and wondered what no-kill meant.

"He is fourteen weeks old. Good day, and thank you."

Hands suddenly grasped Tiger, and pulled him out of the box. Without a word to him, the woman his mother called Momma turned and left the building, taking the crate with her. The noise of barking dogs and wailing cats assailed Tiger's ears, and he shivered with fear. Tiger mewled, and the stranger stroked his back.

"Poor kitty. It is so sad when people dump kittens like this. No real good reason. Sheesh -- she couldn't keep one more cat? I don't understand it at all. Well, at least she didn't dump you on the roadside. Come, big boy, we'll get you settled in," the stranger murmured, as she placed Tiger in a box made of wire. He saw through its mesh sides with ease, surprised to see another enclosure below him. A small litterbox sat in the back corner, and empty food bowls rested at the front. Tiger sat down on the cool plexiglass flooring, shivering. He resisted crying for his mother, trying to be brave, but dread permeated his whole body. He stared straight ahead, aware of cats in cages on either side of him. Below, a litter of very young kittens romped. He glanced down, filled with a yearning to join them.

"Hey, kid," a voice to his right meowed in growling tones. Tiger turned his head, coming face to face with a young black tomcat with a notched ear.

"Me?" Tiger meowed back, ears erect as he minced across the floor to the mesh that separated him from the black cat. His tail rose above his back in friendly greeting, curving, as always, like a huge candy cane. He twitched, trying to straighten it, but it only flopped over, creating another furry hook.

"Yeah, kid, you," the black tom grumbled, his piercing yellow eyes full of curiosity and belligerence.

"I am Tiger, a Maine Coon cat," Tiger replied, puffing with kitten pride.

"Ha! So noble a name for so tiny a tom."

"I'm not a tom." Tiger blinked with surprise. He purred. "I'm not grown up yet."

"Oh, no?" the black cat growled. "If you are more than 6 moon cycles old, you're a tom."

"But I am just three moon cycles old," Tiger retorted, slanting his ears back with indignation. He sat down, gazing at the black cat.

"Three?" The tomcat lifted his ears with surprise.

"Yes, three," Tiger insisted.

The black tom scented the air carefully, and relaxed, his expression friendly.

"I smell no tomcat scent from you. You are what you say -- a mere kitten."

"A *strong* kitten!" Tiger puffed again with pride, and stood up.

"Yes, perhaps," the tomcat sneezed with feline mirth. "You're a big one all right."

Tiger trotted forward, and pressed his nose against the mesh.

"Friends?"

"Sure, kid," the black tom purred. "You can call me Black."

"O.K., Black."

"Want to hear a story, kid?"

"Yes!" Tiger settled back onto his rump.

"Well, many sun cycles ago, when I was just a very young tom, my owner put me in a place like this, right after I began spraying to mark my territory."

"You've been here for sun cycles?" Tiger cocked his head. "Spraying?"

"No, no," Black chuckled. "This was a different place, a small building, far from here. You will know spraying when you get older, young one. Anyway, one morning when they opened the cage to feed me, I leaped out."

"You did?"

"Yes, and I ran and ran, all over the place, until another human entered the shelter. When that door opened, I escaped. I raced until I ran out of breath. I was frightened at first, out all alone, with no human to feed me."

"Weak tom, you are, Black!" A sharp voice interrupted them. "Wasting time on a goofy kitten. Dumb kitten. Big stupid kitten."

Tiger whirled to face the cage on his left. A white female with black markings glared at him. Baleful green eyes bore into him.

"I'm not dumb," Tiger said.

"Big dopey kitten, who knows nothing of this world," the female spat. Tiger flattened his ears, and hissed back at her in defiance and hurt.

"I'm only a kitten. I can't know such things."

"Faugh! You are dopier than most, clumsy big-pawed idiot."

"Am not!" Tiger wailed.

"Kid, ignore her. She is just an cranky old queen."

Tiger shook himself, and slowly turned his back on her. He sat down, ignoring her continuing insults, and listened to Black's stories of the tomcat's days on the streets. Tiger's heart pounded with a mix of fear and excitement, until the lights shut off, leaving the shelter in the dark. He stepped onto the old towel the shelter people supplied for a bed. He lay still, noticing things he missed earlier. The odor of many litterboxes lingered in the air. He suddenly understood what Black meant earlier by spraying, when he saw a grey tabby tom across the aisle mark the back of his cage with urine. The pungent scents of tomcats spraying their meager territories hung in the air. Black, too, joined in, marking the back of his cage, growling insults at the tom across the room. Tiger flattened his ears, not understanding the exchanges of anger and strife, nor the need to pass water in any other place but the litterbox. He wanted to ask Black why the tom sprayed, but found no courage to interrupt the tomcat, as Black paced his cage, trading insults with the other tomcats.

The smell of strong disinfectants mingled with the odor of dogs and humans. The food which lay in the bowl inside his cage smelled stale. He nibbled at it earlier, liking the crunchy texture, but its bland taste repelled him. His hunger moved him again, and he rose to eat the dry food. He drank plenty of water, then lay back on his bedding, and closed his eyes, yawning. The dogs quieted in the darkened building, and cat talk dominated the airwaves.

"Little clumsy mongrel kitten," the cranky female suddenly snarled at him. "You are no Maine Coon."

"I am, too!" Tiger bared his teeth in a defiant hiss of indignation. "My mama and papa were. So am I."

"Ha!" the female curled her lips in a derisive hiss. The cap of black on her head wrinkled as she laid back her ears. "And I am some Queen Angora!"

"I wouldn't know it if you were," Tiger sat up, cocking his head, his voice rising with pride. "But I know I am a Maine Coon."

"Faugh!" she growled. "Look at you! Cow-hocked, splay-footed, no ruff to speak of. You're a misfit."

"You're so mean. Why?" Tiger flattened his ears with sudden shame. "Why do you hate me?"

"Cappie, leave the poor kid alone." Black's sharp snarl turned Tiger around on his bedding. "Ignore her, kid. She is jealous. It's obvious you're a Maine Coon. She knows nothing."

"She doesn't?"

"No," Black rumbled. "I've seen Maine Coons. You are one. Don't fret. Sleep."

"You're right." Tiger curled up against the mesh, feeling the warmth of his new friend's body. He turned his back to the snobbish female, and fell asleep.

# CHAPTER 3: BLACK

Tiger woke to terrified feline squalling. He scrabbled to his feet as a white-clad human pulled the cranky female from her cage. The human held the hissing, squirming queen firmly, and walked into the rear of the building.

"Where is she going?" Tiger asked. "Strangers taking her to a new home?'

"No, kid," Black answered, his raspy voice subdued. "She is going to the Big Sleep."

"Big Sleep?"

"Yes. After a time of living here, if no stranger comes to adopt us, we are brought back there, and . . . and . . ." Black faltered. Dread smoldered in Tiger's heart at his friend's tone.

"And?" Tiger mewled, afraid to hear the answer.

"And put to death."

"Death?" Tiger cocked his head in confusion.

"Yes, death," Black said, regarding him with fearful yellow eyes. "The final sleep. You never wake up. You never see, hear, scent, or touch anything again."

Tiger sat, stunned, recalling his mother's anguished cries when her human momma took him from her and abandoned him in this building.

"What kind of place is this?" Tiger mewed.

"A shelter for those of us without homes." Black laid back his ears. "I have been to too many. Some are good, some horrible. This one is not terrible, except for the Big Sleep."

"So -- so, Cappie isn't coming back? She isn't going home with a good stranger?"

"No, kid, she isn't." Black lashed his tail.

"How awful." Tiger curled his tail tight to his body and shivered. "She was mean, but -- but she . . ."

"I know," Black interrupted. "She does not deserve to die. None of us do, but they run out of room."

"They can't make more room?"

"Sometimes, but most times they have way too many of us here. You are lucky. You are a kitten. Most strangers want kittens." Black lay down, hunched in misery. "I, however, am a full-grown tomcat. Unless I can escape, I will die here. And it looks like escape will be very difficult."

"Oh, Black!" Tiger wailed, and curled up against the mesh, trembling with fear for his friend and for himself. He watched Cappie's cage. Very little time passed before a human placed another cat into the empty cage. The fluffy grey-and-white kitten with a very short muzzle mewled in fear. Tiger rose, and walked across his cage, feeling deep empathy for the scared kitten.

"Hi! My name is Tiger! I am a Maine Coon!"

"Hi!" the fluffy kitten meowed, his tail rising straight in eager delight. He frolicked to the mesh. "I am Puff, a Persian."

"Glad to meet you." Tiger's tail rose, falling over in a long furry hook.

"What a long pretty tail," Puff meowed. "Mine is so short."

Puff whirled, trying to pin his little tail beneath his chubby forepaws. Tiger laughed with delight, and copied his pudgy friend. Tiger engaged Puff in play most of that morning, until a shelter worker removed Puff from the cage. Scared, Puff mewled as the worker handed Puff to a smiling stranger, who placed Puff in a pretty carrier, cooing baby talk at him.

"Lucky tyke," Black commented, startling Tiger. "He is going to a good home."

"Bye, Puff!" Tiger called out to him. "Don't be scared!"

Tiger sat down, watching the bright carrier swing gently from its owner's hand as it carried Puff to a new life. Tiger missed his friend, and mewed his unhappiness. A shelter worker came over, and opened

Puff's cage. With strong-smelling disinfectant, the busy human cleaned the enclosure. Tiger wrinkled his nose in distaste. In moments, Puff's scent dwindled on the air currents. Tiger sat on his bedding, watching as the shelter worker placed a new occupant in the cage. The old short-haired calico curled up on her bedding, and moaned. Tiger rose, and pressed his nose against the mesh. The old cat reminded him of his sister Callie.

"Hello! My name is Tiger. Who are you?"

The old one turned bleary, clouded, green eyes to him, and uttered a soft wail of distress.

"Leave her," Black said softly. "She's grieving. I'd bet my dinner her owner died."

"Oh, oh!" Tiger sat down hard on the plexiglass. "So-so s-s-orry."

The elder lifted her aged head, her ears quivering, her eyes searching.

"Thank yee, Youngin'," she purred raggedly. "I shall follow mee momma soon. Soon."

The elder dropped her head and curled up, ignoring her food and water. Tiger returned to his bedding, his eyes on the elderly calico. Over the next two days, she moved not a muscle unless forced to do so by a shelter worker. Tiger settled into a routine of mealtimes and sleep, enjoying the company of Black.

On his fourth day at the shelter, Tiger woke to Black's restless pacing. He stretched, yawned, then sat up.

"What's wrong?"

"Fifth day, fifth day," Black muttered in sad little chirrups.

"Fifth day?" Tiger asked. Black halted his pacing, regarding Tiger with wide eyes.

"My time is up, kid," Black mewled like a kitten.

"You mean . . ." Tiger clicked his teeth in a chatter, stopping further words.

"Yes," Black said, and resumed pacing. A shelter worker placed food in Black's bowl. Black leaped for the open cage door, but the worker swiftly shut it in his face. Black yowled in anguish. All day, Black walked the perimeter of his cage, wailing softly, ignoring Tiger's pleas for a story. Tiger wished to make Black stop pacing and lie down, but no matter what Tiger asked, Black ignored him. The scent of his dread struck terror into Tiger's very bones. Tiger cried every time a shelter worker came near the cages.

At day's end, a white-clad worker strode to Black's cage and pulled open the door. Black tried to bolt, but the worker grasped him firmly by the scruff of his neck. He howled, snarled, and slashed at empty air with unsheathed claws.

"Nooooo!" Tiger cried, as the worker carried Black toward the back of the quiet shelter. Responding feline wails answered Tiger's voice, and dogs barked.

"Bye, Tiger!" Black keened. "Tiger! Stay cage-front! Get adopted before this time tomorrow! Or you, too, will follow me!"

Black's voice faded as the worker carried him down the dark hallway to the rear of the building. Tiger strained his ears, able to hear his friend's howls, wails, and hisses. A door slammed shut, but Tiger still heard his friend's wailing. Suddenly, human cursing joined Black's terrified caterwauling. Tiger's ears quivered with each new sound. Humans shouted. Black shrieked, and metal clatter echoed from behind the closed door. The noise ceased after a few moments and Tiger let out a sad mew.

Rearing up against the mesh, he craned his neck, trying to get a better view of the doorway at the end of the long shadowy corridor. He meowed in fear, his vocalization resembling the bleating of a lamb more than a kitten's cry. Tiger dropped back down, and curled on his bed, trembling. He looked toward the old calico.

"Why? Why did they take Black away?" Tiger asked in grief-stricken tones. The old one stirred for the first time in days, and turned cloudy eyes to him.

"So sorry, Youngin'," she meowed softly. "Such a strong young tom. It should've been me, should have been me."

She laid her head back down, and Tiger curled up on his bed. The night passed slowly.

## CHAPTER 4: FIFTH DAY

Tiger slept restlessly until sunrise slanted bright rays into the front of the shelter. Tiger rose and paced, until he recalled Black's last words: stay cage-front. Tiger sat down by the mesh, and watched everything that morning. He nibbled at his breakfast, but found it tasteless and unappealing. Tiger returned to his spot at the front of his cage. Strange humans sauntered up and down the aisles all day, and Tiger drew himself up proudly. Not one gave him more than a mere glance. The sun retracted its beams as it rounded the building, and Tiger shifted his forefeet nervously. A shelter worker in white approached his cage, and Tiger froze with fear. He uttered a soft "meh" of dread. The human opened the cage.

"So sorry, so sorry, little one, but we have to do this." The worker's voice shook as she reached for Tiger. Tiger sensed her sadness, and mewed.

"Wait!" A voice from across the room halted the worker. Her hand dropped to her side.

Tiger sat, trying to be brave. The other worker hurried toward the cage, followed by a tall dark-haired man. Tiger looked at the man, and sat, ears erect, trying not to show his fear.

"Yes, Maine Coon," the man muttered. "Yes, no doubts."

The man gently took Tiger from the cage. Tiger purred, his heart filled with desperate hope. The man smiled at him.

"My wife will love him," he said. "I'll take him."

"Oh, thank you, sir," one worker smiled. "Your generosity just gave him a new lease on life."

"You mean he was going to be put down?" the man scowled, his strong arms holding Tiger protectively. Tiger kneaded the man's sleeve. "He's just a kitten!"

"Yes, I know," the worker answered apologetically. "It's been a heavy season for unwanted kittens and strays. The management is sticking by the five-day grace period for all our occupants, even kittens." The girl inhaled, and Tiger saw tears in her eyes. "Sometimes I really hate this job."

"Well, this is one kitten that you won't have to euthanize." The man turned away from the cage, then strode toward the front of the shelter. Tiger snuggled against the man, until a worker took him and placed him in a cardboard box. He tried to mew, but nothing came out. The box suddenly moved, and Tiger heard strong footfalls as his box swung gently to and fro. He thought of the day a stranger adopted Puff.

The box stopped moving when the man set him down on the seat of a red car. Tiger sniffed the air. New scents and sounds assailed his senses. He smelled strange cats and humans, as well as odors that flickered in his memory until he remembered the day he arrived at the shelter. A rumble shook him and his box, then suddenly his whole world moved again, gyrating gently. He peeked through the holes in the box, and saw the tall man sitting beside him. Music blared loudly from somewhere outside his box, and the man sang along. Tiger listened, relaxing as the journey grew long.

Finally, the vehicle stopped, and Tiger's box once again swung in the man's grasp. Through the holes in the cardboard carrier, Tiger saw many strange and wonderful things. Enticing scents wafted on the air currents as the man brought him into a strange house, not unlike his early home. Tiger's heart swelled with hope. His carrier thumped to the floor, and Tiger heard a strange woman's voice mingle with the man's. Unfamiliar cat scents tingled his nose. Suddenly, the top to his carrier opened, and the woman gazed down at him, tears in her eyes. Sadness radiated from her, as well as shocked surprise. Tiger met her gaze, his fear diminishing.

"Oh, he's so cute, but so big," she said. The man handed her papers, and Tiger watched her eyes widen. "He's only 3 months old? He looks like he's at least 5!"

She reached in, and lifted Tiger out of the box. Tiger purred, then surveyed the large room, liking the four huge windows that allowed golden sunlight to bathe the room. The woman placed Tiger on the white linoleum floor, and he gazed around. The odor of a strange female cat hung strong in the air. The old scent of a male cat mingled with the female's, but Tiger knew the male left that behind many days ago. He stepped forward, and explored the paneled room, sniffing every corner. The light pad of paws attracted his attention. He turned from his investigations, and met the shocked green eyes of a pretty blue-cream tortoiseshell cat.

"No!" she hissed. "Not another one! I will not tolerate this!"

She marched up to him, tail puffed with outrage, anger in every step.

"You'll never replace him! Never!" the blue-cream snarled, and raised a paw. Tiger backed against a chair, fear and astonishment rushing through him before indignation doused his dread.

"I am Tiger!" he retorted, baring needle fangs, raising a golden paw in defiance. Black tufts fluttered between his spreading toes as his long claws flashed out.

"You'll never replace Demon! Never!" the female hissed, swatting empty air.

"Mandee-Mau!" the woman cried, and Tiger registered the name of his assailant.

"I don't want to," he hissed, swatting back. Mandee hissed again, whirled, and ran upstairs.

"You never will," her plaintive meow echoed down the stairwell. Tiger watched, and then looked at the two humans. Both gaped in astonishment.

"Did you see that?" the man asked.

"Yes, amazing! He stood up to Mandee!"

"He's a little tiger," the man chuckled. "I think we should call him Khan, like Shere-Khan from *The Jungle Book*."

"What a great name," the woman agreed, scooping Tiger into her arms. "Yes, we will call you Khan from now on."

Tiger purred, thinking his new name so grand. He mulled it over in his mind, enjoying the attention of his new momma and poppy.

On the following afternoon, his momma carried him to the bathroom where Poppy sat next to the tub. The sound of running water echoed in the room, and instinctive fear filled Khan. Momma handed him to Poppy, and, as Momma shut off the faucet, Poppy slowly lowered Khan into the water.

"Noooooo!" Khan wailed, his kitten voice shrill with sudden panic. "What are you doing to me?? Noooo!" Khan squalled. He tried leaping free of Poppy's grasp, but Poppy held him firmly, while Momma lathered him up with soap.

"Stay still, sweetie. You need a nice bath. Doesn't it feel good?" Momma scooped up warm water from the tub, and slowly poured it over Khan, rinsing the soap away. Water trickled into Khan's eyes, and terror swept through him.

"Nooo! No feel good! Scared!" He flailed wildly, and to his horror, his feet slipped out from under him. Water closed over his head, stinging his eyes, stabbing up his nose, and clogging his ears. He cried out in panic, and water flooded his mouth. He struggled to breathe, desperately trying to gain any hold on the slick tub with his claws. His heart hammered in his chest.

"Oh my God!" he heard his new momma gasp. A strong hand grasped him by the neck and hauled him free of the deadly water. Khan coughed away the fluid and wailed his terror.

"You poor sweet baby!" Momma cried, her voice shaking. "O.K., Bathtime is over."

She reached for him with a soft towel, and Poppy placed him in Momma's embrace. She wrapped the towel around him, and hugged him to her chest.

"I'm so sorry," Poppy said, stroking Khan's wet head. Khan shivered, and as his dread ebbed, he realized Poppy and Momma did not mean to dunk him. Momma carried him into the livingroom and sat on the sofa, cuddling him, keeping him warm. He shivered, with both cold and fear, but soon relaxed as Momma's loving grasp warmed him. He knew Momma and Poppy never meant to hurt him, but just the thought of a tub of water sent dread into his very bones. He put it out of his mind, and fell asleep, feeling loved and warm.

As time ticked by, Khan thrust the bathtime scare into the depths of his memory, and adapted to his new home. He played with the abundance of toys, and ate the wonderful foods, but he sensed Momma's deep sadness. Mandee disdained him, and spoke no further to him. At times, while he played quietly in the dining room, he heard his momma crying in the next room. A deep grief permeated her presence, reminding him of the elderly cat left behind at the shelter. He wondered if

Momma regretted his arrival, and, as he played, loneliness filled him. He missed his mother, siblings, and Black.

One night, a thunderstorm rumbled and flashed outside the old house, vibrating it to its stone foundation. Startled and frightened, Khan sought out his momma, and huddled on top of her feet. He looked up, and tried to meow, but nothing emerged from his throat. Momma looked down.

"Awww, my poor little Meathead. Are you scared?" His momma picked him up, then cuddled him to her chest. He purred.

"Do you ever meow, little one?" she asked.

"My meow is weak," he explained, despite knowing she did not understand cat-speak.

"My, what a strong purr," she murmured to him, and held him. He wanted so much to push away the sadness that surrounded her. He purred louder, and looked up, blinking, hoping she at least understood a kitten kiss when she saw it. She smiled, and hugged him, but, even as she displayed such affection, Khan's momma continued to radiate grief, and, some days, Khan felt alone. He endured it by playing quietly, resting on a chair, and purring with all his strength to his momma whenever she cuddled him. Despite all his resolve, he felt lonely and scared, and wished for someone to play with.

## CHAPTER 5: PHANTOM

One day, Momma came into the house, carrying something small. Khan scented the air, watching from the comfort of the sofa.

"I hope you like him, Khan. Be a good boy," his momma said, as she set a pewter-grey tabby with black stripes and stark white markings on the slate of the foyer. The tiny kitten with enormous ears crouched in fear.

"Mama! Mama!" he mewed. Khan leaped from the sofa, and rushed into the hallway, joyous to see another kitten. Behind him, Mandee hissed in scorn.

"Oh, no! Not another one!" She whirled, and ran upstairs.

"Hellooo!" he cried in glee, twittering with joy. "I am Khan!"

"Mama!" the kitten mewled, but let Khan touch his nose in greeting.

"Please, please, play with me," Khan pleaded, tapping the new kitten with a big paw.

"Oh, oh! Mama! You're so big! I'm scared!" the kitten whimpered, crouching in terror, his eyes wide with dread. Khan touched the tiny ball of fluff, barely a third his size, then flopped on his side, inviting the baby to play. "Please play with me."

"I'm scared. I want my mama!"

Khan's momma scooped up the terrified kitten, and placed him on the sofa. There, the kitten responded to human contact, relaxing, and enjoying the petting. Khan jumped up on the sofa, and touched the kitten with his nose.

"Why won't you play with me?"

"Nooo! Too big! Scared!" The kitten scurried behind Poppy.

"Aww, poor Phantom," Momma said quietly. "Khan, don't worry. It will take time."

Khan waited. Each day when baby Phantom visited, Khan tried his best to show the tiny kitten affection and playfulness. Every night, Phantom left, returning next door to his mother and siblings, leaving an empty spot in Khan's heart. On the fifth day, though he quailed at first when Khan approached him, Phantom stood his ground and sniffed noses with Khan.

"Not hurt me?"

"Never," Khan answered. The kitten ran, his tiny tail sticking straight up as he raced into the next room.

Khan followed, thundering down the hall in glee. Nimble, swift, and agile, little Phantom led Khan on a merry chase. Khan caught Phantom on the sofa and wrestled him, but one scared cry from his new buddy caused Khan to back off. Phantom uttered little mews of warning and fear, but he wrestled back, escaping to lead the wild race up and down the stairs and all through the house. That night, much to Khan's delight, Phantom did not leave to rejoin his mother and siblings at the house next door.

"Why?" Khan asked the tiny kitten, as they ran down the hall. "Why did you never fear Momma and Poppy, yet you were so scared of me? I'd never hurt you."

"I always know Momma," Phantom halted, and sat down on the slate. A look of confusion crossed his face. "Just know Momma."

"How?"

"I remember Momma, always," Phantom answered, his face furrowed with concentration.

"I don't understand," Khan said, flicking his ears. "I didn't always know Momma. How can you?"

"I just know," Phantom answered, his blue eyes bright. Something flickered in those eyes, a brief flash of gold-green. "I remember, when I first see things, and I play with sisters. I see Momma. I stop, and climb on my mama's momma. I stare at Momma, and in my head, I think, my momma, she your momma, yes, my momma."

"She your momma?" Khan lashed his tail. "How old were you?"

"Just able to see things." Phantom cocked his head, slanting back his huge ears. 'It sound like another voice, like someone tell me 'she your momma.' I stare at Momma a long time. She look at me. She know, too. That why I here."

"I don't understand."

"It just be," Phantom stood up, tail in the air. "Play?"

"Yes!" Khan beamed a feline smile.

Khan followed his little athletic friend on every excursion. Phantom climbed the dining room drapes, hanging from the rod, his eyes full of mischief. He looked down at Khan.

"Can't get me!"

"Yes, I can!" Khan retorted, and reared up, hooking his claws into the lacy curtains. He struggled to haul himself upward, but managed to swing to and fro, front claws in the fabric, back feet on the ground.

"Too big!" Phantom chirped in delight, until quick footfalls stopped both their movements.

"Oh, my God! Hon! Come look at this!" Poppy's deep tones, full of shock and amusement, echoed in the room. Momma appeared beside Poppy before either Phantom or Khan reacted to Poppy's voice. Both humans broke out into uproarious laughter. Phantom launched himself from the rod, and hit the floor running. Khan twisted free of the curtain, and followed his buddy. No scolding followed him up the hall. Just laughter.

"They are laughing at us!" Khan sat down on the landing.

"Not at us, but you!" Phantom twittered with mirth. "You should have seen yourself!"

"I can't help that I'm so much bigger," Khan grumbled. "But you're growing, too. Someday, you will not be able to get up there."

Phantom suddenly ran up the stairs, tail aloft. Khan leaped after him, forgetting the incident.

Phantom grew swiftly, as did Khan, and before they knew it, both developed into huge young toms. Neither understood the changes beginning in their bodies, but the wrestling grew increasingly rough, and, too many times, Khan sat back, apologizing to his pal. One time, Khan grabbed Phantom's nape in his jaws, straddling him, confused by his actions, yet driven to it by some deep instinct. Phantom spun underneath him, snarling, and lay on his back.

"Get off of me!" he spat, and wiggled out from under Khan, then jumped on Khan's back. Khan reacted in alarm, rearing up and rolling over.

"Stop that!"

"See how it feels?" Phantom growled, pouncing on him.

"I'm sorry," he lamented.

"You always are!" Phantom glared back from bluish-green eyes. His short fur bristled from a long, lean, tall frame.

"But I don't like when you jump on my back! Why are you doing that?"

"I don't know," Phantom cocked his head, and sat down. "I don't like it either when you do it. Do you know why you do it?"

"No." Khan sat down, and groomed his own face.

Not long after this argument, Momma whisked Khan and his buddy into a large carrier to see the cat doctor. They huddled against each other during the ride, and old memories raced through Khan's mind, as they always did during car trips. When Momma took Khan and his friend into the Animal Hospital, Phantom wailed in his strident voice.

"Why must Momma take us here?"

"I don't know," Khan cried in his baby-doll meow.

"Now, be good boys," Momma admonished. "You must be neutered."

"What is that?" Phantom yowled, as the carrier swung into motion again. In the exam room, the cat doctor pulled Khan and Phantom from the carrier. Khan trembled as the scents, sights, and sounds assailed his senses. It reminded him of the shelter he came from many moon cycles ago. Momma hugged him and Phantom, then left the room. Khan cried out, and, to his shock, a bellowing meow exploded from his throat. The cat doctor and his assistant carried Khan and his buddy into the back rooms, and placed them in clean cages. Khan meowed inarticulate fear, his wildcat cries causing other animals to meow, bark, or squawk. Phantom joined him, serenading the room with the strident cries of his Siamese ancestors.

Shortly, someone removed Khan and Phantom from their cages, and administered shots. Khan lost the strength in his voice. He squeaked once in fear, recalling Black's words: the Big Sleep. His new momma did this to him? Why? He knew he and Phantom behaved badly many times, but they never meant harm. As he pondered the reasons, the room blackened before his eyes.

Khan slowly woke, smelling the scents of the Animal Hospital. He blinked in the light, and saw that he and Phantom lay back in their cages. What happened? Khan tried to move, and felt some soreness on his behind. The effort to sit up tired him, so he moved his head. Phantom lay still, sleeping. Groggy, Khan waited anxiously to see what happened next.

Later, as daylight waned, someone gently urged Khan and Phantom into the familiar large carrier. Khan blinked as the carrier swung through the brightly lit waiting area. He perked up suddenly, hearing a familiar voice.

"Momma!" he mewled. Momma peeked into the carrier at him.

"You're going home now, my little boys." Momma smiled. Khan endured the car ride, his heart singing. Once inside the house he loved, he staggered out of the carrier. Phantom followed.

"We are back home!"

Time passed from that scary day, and Khan realized trips to the cat doctor did not mean going to the Big Sleep. He and Phantom played like kittens again. Since the visit to the cat doctor, they wrestled, romped, and played, free of animosity and aggression. Phantom always uttered little meows while wrestling, a carryover from those early first days, and Khan laughed at him.

"You are as big as I am now!" he said one morning. "You shouldn't have to cry like a little kitten."

"I can't help it," Phantom blinked a feline smile. "Just like you can't help bellowing like a wildcat at bath time."

"I hate baths." Khan laid back his ears, and pounced on his buddy. Phantom rolled away, and raced up the hall. Khan followed, tail in the air, curved, as always, like a huge furry hook. They wrestled and romped until exhausted, then they snuggled together on the sofa. As moonbeams slanted in the huge window, Khan thought suddenly of Black. Sadness engulfed his soul, and he wished his friend lived here, in this happy house. With a sigh, he fell asleep, and dreamed of his shelter days.

# CHAPTER 6: REUNION

Moon cycles passed quickly, and Leaf Bloom arrived in a rush of warm weather. Open windows beckoned to Khan, and he wistfully watched Phantom patrol the yard. He wondered why Momma did not let him accompany Phantom outdoors.

"You're lucky," he complained to Phantom one sunny morning.

"Momma doesn't think you'll be safe out here," Phantom replied over his shoulder as he ran to the door. "I can take care of myself!"

"So can I," Khan grumbled. "I am as big as you are."

"I know, but remember, you're purebred, like Demon was, and Momma let him out alone. He died very young." Phantom paused at the threshold.

"I won't die," Khan argued.

"You Maine Coons are tunnel-sighted! Get too focused and have no fear of things!" Phantom retorted. "I know you, and you'd let yourself get hit by a car or do something stupid like fall out of a tree because you're too focused on whatever caught your attention."

"I would not!" Khan protested with a growl.

"Yes, you would, and that is why Momma doesn't let you out alone." Phantom finished, and ran outside. Khan stood, staring at the closed door, tail flopping from side to side, but after much thought, realized his friend might be right.

One morning, Momma presented a red contraption to Khan, and fitted it to his body.

"You'll love your harness," Momma assured him. The alien feel of the straps around his belly, chest, and back filled Khan with apprehension, and he flopped on his side. Gentle coaxing and tension on the straps brought Khan outdoors. He forgot the strange straps, and eagerly explored the yard, all under the watchful eye of Momma. Phantom joined him, cavorting around him and Momma.

"This is great!" he cried.

"Yes!" Khan agreed. Suddenly, an older black tomcat came into view. He crossed the yard, trotting toward Phantom's birthplace, the house next door. Phantom spied him first, and puffed up. Khan watched, astonished by his best friend's sudden anger.

"This is my yard," he growled.

Khan saw the stranger, and, tail over his back, he trotted toward the black cat. He never understood why other cats reacted with aggression when meeting, either for the first time or the tenth. Phantom and Mandee thought his behavior quite odd, and told him so often enough, but he did not care. He viewed all as friends unless they proved otherwise. So far, except for poor Cappie, back at the shelter, all cats eventually reciprocated his trust. He inhaled the stranger's scent, but the black cat bolted, hissing.

"Who are you? You're huge! Get away from me!"

Khan stared in shock and recognition as the voice and scent registered in his brain.

"Black!" Khan's call rang out. The black tom turned, surprise in his eyes.

"You know my old name?" the tom stood, ears flat, body tense.

"Yes!" Khan strained against his harness, tail up, whiskers forward.

"He trespasses," Phantom growled from behind Khan. "He likes to defy me every chance he gets."

"I live here, too," the black tom growled in protest.

"This is my yard! Yours is over there!" Phantom hissed, hair raised, tail puffed, as he crouched in attack mode.

Khan turned a quick head. "Please, no! He's an old friend, please. Stay there."

"For you, I will." Phantom obeyed, sitting down, but never moving his eyes from the black tomcat. "You are crazy to trust anyone." Khan ignored Phantom.

"I know you, Black! Don't you remember me?" Khan meowed in his silly baby-doll voice.

The black cat cautiously approached, and touched noses with Khan. His body language changed in an instant. Tail up, eyes wide, whiskers forward, he sat down.

"Tiger? Little Tiger?" Black sniffed Khan again. "It is you! Great moon cycles, you have grown so much!"

"I have," Khan said with pride, then sobered, remembering the last time he saw Black. "How? How is it you're here? I thought -- I thought they brought you to the Big Sleep."

"They tried," Black sneezed his mirth. "I fought, getting my claws behind and into the big gloves they wear on her arms, and I latched on to her, clawing and biting anything I touched. She screamed, and cursed me, but I wiggled out of her grasp. I ran and ran, shrieking at the top of my lungs, eluding her attempts to recapture me, until someone opened a door to see what was happening. I raced out, and ran until I found an open window, then clawed through the screening. I don't know where in the shelter I was, and I didn't care.

I got out." Black sobered. "I ran for days, not caring where, just to get as far away from there as I could. Then, I got so hungry I had to find food."

"How did you do that?"

"In garbage dumps, and sometimes a kind human would put out food. But someone always came with traps and nets, so I'd run again. Then I wandered into this area, and hung around the lake down the hill for a while. Saw many cats roaming, and decided to come up into this neighborhood. So many kind humans put out food. Nobody came with nets and traps, except the one that trapped my sick friend a few mooncycles ago. I was upset with that, but our mommas only wanted to help him, but he was too sick."

"Who was he?" Khan asked.

"Your momma called him Ghost, and fed him."

"He was your friend?" Phantom asked, eyes baleful. "He knew not to come near me."

"Yes, I met him when I came up the hill." Black answered, acknowledging Phantom's retort by flicking an ear backward. He said his family abandoned him mooncycles ago. Poor old guy. When our mommas got the trap to catch him I almost ran away, but logic prevailed when I realized they wanted to help him and adopt him. But he was very very sick and went to the Big Sleep." Black glanced over his back, then glared at Phantom. "Your mama's momma took me in. I live there now. With your mother and sisters. Why do you hate me?"

"Yes, why do you?" Mandee strolled up next to Black. "You know he is my friend. And poor Ghost was no threat."

"I-I-I don't like trespassers," Phantom meowed a pathetic excuse. "And he was sick! We could get sick, too"

"You let your mother go anywhere, even in your house." Black growled.

"He is my friend," Khan pleaded with his buddy. "Don't hate him."

"If he is your friend, he's mine, too," Phantom capitulated, but his ears lay flat in silent defiance. Khan knew Phantom agreed only to make him happy, but felt unsettled Phantom never told him of his life outdoors.

"Good. No sense fighting," Mandee said.

"Ha! Like you don't attack my mama when she comes over for a snack!" Phantom snapped back at Mandee.

"I only remind her I am Queen of our home, and don't really hurt her." Mandee glanced over into the next yard, where Phantom's petite patched-tabby mother walked along the fence, ignoring everyone. "She forgets sometimes this is my house."

Khan listened in surprise, then noticed how Black watched Mandee move.

"You know Black?"

"I have since he arrived here." Mandee sat down. The sun shone on her blue-creme fur, and it sparkled with a silvery sheen.

"But I have never scented him on you," Khan flicked his ears back, baring the tips of his fangs to Phantom. "Nor on you!"

"He knows better than to touch me," Mandee answered, mirth in her growl. "As do both of you."

"I sure do," Khan agreed

Phantom widened his eyes, and flattened his ears. Mandee laughed, then rose to her feet. She padded up the lawn. Black looked after her wistfully.

"Ah, if only she and I could dance by moonlight. What a fine queen she would have been. But she has no understanding at all." Black sighed. Khan cocked his head in confusion.

"Queen? You mean she isn't?" Khan snorted. "She acts like Queen of All Cats."

"Ah, young one, you were neutered young, like Mandee, thus you don't know what you miss. In a way, you are lucky. But a queen is a female who can bear kittens, and a tom is a male that can sire kittens. I am no longer really a tomcat."

"I don't understand." Khan twitched his whiskers. "You are still big and strong."

"Yes, as are both of you." Black smiled at him and Phantom. "But you will never be toms. Little Tiger, you will never know the joy of pursuing a queen, and winning her from suitors."

"I don't understand what you are saying, but it sounds fun." Khan touched Black's nose, and changed the subject. "Call me Khan. It is my new name."

"Strong name." Black blinked his eyes in approval. "They call me Black Satin, or Satin for short, but you can call me Black if you like."

"Which do you like?"

"Either is fine. I am glad to have a home. It matters not what they call me." Black stood up. "I must be off. Dinner awaits me. Well-met, young Khan. Good to see you again."

"So glad you did not have to go to the Big Sleep."

"So am I, young Khan, so am I!" Black laughed, as he sauntered toward his home.

Khan watched for a long time, unable to believe his senses. Then he recalled Phantom knew Black lived out here, and returned a sad gaze to his best buddy. "Why don't you tell me of these things?"

"I don't know," Phantom turned, and groomed his tail, then said, "guess I didn't think you cared about what goes on out here."

"You lie! I always wanted to come out here!"

"Well, " Phantom heaved a big sigh. "I didn't want you to come out and get hurt or killed like Demon, so I didn't tell you so you wouldn't get excited and try to come out on your own. But Momma solved the problem! Forgive me?"

Khan glared at Phantom for several heartbeats before relaxing.

"Yes, I do. Now that I come out here, too. I wish you would be nicer to Black."

"He and I don't see eye to eye, but I'll try for your sake," Phantom purred. Khan eyed his buddy, knowing again, Phantom only placated him with those words. Wanting to put any strife out of his head, Khan glanced up at Momma, and lifted his tail. He bleated.

"Love me? Love me?"

To his surprise, she picked him up, cuddled him, and carried him in for dinnertime. Phantom followed, tail straight up with excitement, and Khan blinked his eyes in a feline smile.

"What is so funny?" Phantom asked.

"You and food! I'll bet there isn't a cat around for miles that can eat as much as you do."

Phantom merely purred with inner pride. Momma bent over, and unbuckled Khan's harness. Foreboding washed into him as Momma's scent entered his nose again. This time, something smelled wrong.

## CHAPTER 7: MISSING MOMMA

As Leaf Bloom turned to Leaf Fall, Khan watched and worried as Momma fell ill. Each day she weakened, turning pale. Khan scented blood and sickness. One warm evening, Momma stumbled to the sofa after a hurried trip to the bathroom. She crumpled onto the blankets and pillows, breathing hard.

"You all right?" Poppy asked, worry in his voice.

"No. I barely have the strength to get from the bathroom."

"Are you going back to the doctor tomorrow?"

"Yes. I think she has to change the medication back," Momma answered in a labored whisper. "If she doesn't, I think I'm going to bleed to death."

"Just stay still and calm," Poppy said. "Conserve your strength."

He took her hand. Khan watched the exchange, fear and worry racing his heart. He jumped on a chair, all thoughts of the disagreements with his best friend gone from his mind, joining Phantom, who snoozed against a pillow.

"What is wrong with Momma?" Khan asked, pawing his best friend.

"I don't know," Phantom answered, lifting his head. "But it smells wrong."

"I know, and I'm scared." Khan lay down beside Phantom, and kept his eyes on Momma every moment possible.

A few days later, Poppy helped Momma out of the house. Khan watched, standing in the hallway, forlorn, feeling helpless.

"I don't like this," he mewled to Phantom. Phantom sat beside him on the dark cool slate.

"I don't either. Poppy should be going to work."

"He may be going shopping with Momma," Mandee suggested, coming down the steps.

"Momma left her purse here," Phantom argued, glancing back into the dining room. Momma's black purse sat in its usual place by the phone.

"Maybe they are going on a trip?" Mandee tilted her head.

"No, Poppy did not pack a bag. Only Momma did." Khan meowed in agitation. Outside, the car started up. Khan bounded up the stairs, and jumped into the window at the top of the stairwell. He watched the red car drive away.

"He's right," Phantom said. "Momma brings her purse on those trips."

"Not always," Mandee reminded them. "She sometimes takes smaller purses and leaves the big one home. She did the same this time."

"But Poppy didn't pack. So why?" Khan asked, staring at the spot he last saw the car.

"Maybe Poppy is taking her to a human doctor, like Momma takes us to a cat doctor," Mandee suggested. Khan did not turn his head, but relaxed his ears.

"Yes, maybe that's it."

"That makes sense," Phantom agreed, and Khan glanced at them. Mandee's green eyes shone with worry. Khan saw his own anxieties reflected in his pal's sea-green eyes. Patiently, he waited for the car to return. Mandee left them shortly, but Phantom stayed with Khan until his stomach growled. He flicked his whiskers forward.

"I need a snack." Phantom left to eat. Khan waited, and, finally, after dark, the car returned. Khan stood up in the window, excited, until he noticed that only Poppy got out of the car. As Poppy headed for the door, Khan ran down the steps. Poppy opened the door and walked in. Khan greeted him with querulous soft meows. Poppy looked down, and smiled. Mandee hurried in from the livingroom as Poppy entered the kitchen, meowing incessantly. Phantom lifted his head from the food dish, and meowed in strident tones.

"Where's Momma?" all three asked over and over again. Poppy, not understanding catspeak, offered food, treats, water, and catnip. Finally, Poppy stood in the middle of the kitchen, exasperated, and said, "What do you silly cats want?"

"Where's Momma?" Khan asked, rubbing Poppy's legs. Mandee and Phantom did likewise. Mandee reared up on her back legs, her meows beseeching. Phantom's strident voice rose in volume. Poppy gazed at them a moment before his scowl softened.

"I'm sorry, guys. Momma is not here." Poppy gave them each a loving stroke, and disappeared into the bathroom.

"We know that!" Khan mewed, following Poppy. Phantom and Mandee trailed him. Poppy stepped into the shower and turned on the water. He closed the glass doors.

"Where is Momma?" Phantom meowed. Poppy did not answer, but began singing. Patiently, Khan waited until Poppy finished and grabbed a towel to dry off.

"Where is Momma?"

"Silly cats," Poppy said softly. "Momma will be gone a while."

"Why?"

Poppy only patted Khan's head, and put on his night clothes.

"He is trying to hide his worry," Phantom said from the doorway. "But I sense it."

"So do I," Khan agreed. All evening, they tried to pry answers from Poppy, but he only patted their heads. Khan led his companions up the stairs when Poppy retired to bed. He sat in front of the closed door.

"Where is Momma?" he mewled like a kitten.

"Is Momma inside?" Phantom asked.

"No," Mandee answered, "but Poppy must know. We have to make him tell us."

Mandee meowed a sad wail. Phantom raised his Siamese voice, bellowing out his queries. Khan joined in with soft baby-doll cries. Mandee scratched at the door. It jiggled in its frame. Suddenly, they heard movement inside the room. Poppy flung back the door. Mandee raced in, Phantom on her heels. Khan ambled in, heading for the bed. He leaped up, purring between his soft queries.

"Where is Mommmmaaaaaaaaaaaaaaaa?" Phantom howled.

"See? She isn't here," Poppy admonished. "Let me get some sleep, guys. Now, scoot. Out, out, out!"

Khan ran out behind his companions, and the door shut behind them. Khan sat a moment, watching the door, then rose to his feet.

"He will get mad if we do that again. I'm going downstairs."

"Me, too." Phantom turned, and hurried down the steps. Khan followed. Mandee darted past them into the livingroom. She curled up on a chair. Khan trotted to the sofa, jumped up, and settled on the spot where Momma's scent lay strongest. The night ticked by, and, at dawn, Poppy awoke. Mandee and Phantom ran to greet him in the kitchen. Khan waited, not wishing to leave his spot, but soon joined his housemates in badgering Poppy again. Poppy put down their breakfast, and hurried around, getting ready, as he usually did, for work. Khan rubbed against Poppy's legs, almost tripping him when he came out of the bathroom.

"Khan! Stop that," Poppy scolded. "You guys are driving me crazy."

Picking up his lunch and satchel, Poppy left the house. Khan ran to the window in the stairwell. Mandee raced into the livingroom, and leaped onto the sofa. Khan's heart jumped with jealousy.

"No!" Khan protested from his window perch. "That's my spot."

He hurried down the slippery steps and ran to the sofa. Mandee jumped onto the sofa back, ignoring him. She pawed the curtains, trying get behind them.

"Can you see anything?" Khan asked. "Let me see, too!"

Khan joined Mandee on the sofa back, clawing at the heavy drapery. Phantom bounded up on the couch.

"What are you doing?"

Phantom shoved himself between Mandee and Khan. The body contact shocked Mandee. She hissed.

"Don't touch me!" She careened off the sofa back. The drapes caught her, trapping her against the window. Khan jumped down to the cushions, but his hooked claws wrenched him around.

"I'm stuck!" he yowled.

"Let me out!" Mandee wailed. A sudden metallic pop above them froze everyone. A small metal object dropped onto Phantom.

"Run!" he warned, and bolted. Mandee wailed again, trying to free herself. Khan's heart pounded with sudden terror when his claws refused to come free of the curtains. Another pop, and rattling metal echoed in the room. Khan shook his paw and freed his claws, then spun around in a clumsy leap to the floor. The drapes collapsed onto the sofa. Mandee screamed, battled the fabric, and darted out of a fold, streaking from the room. Khan watched as the rod settled across his sleeping spot.

"Poppy is gonna be mad," he said softly. Later that evening, Poppy arrived home late. He immediately noticed the downed drapes.

"What did you cats do today?" he scolded, his tones rumbling with deep annoyance. Poppy returned the curtains to their rightful place. Mandee and Phantom scurried away, but Khan followed Poppy into the kitchen.

"Sorry, sorry," he mewled. That evening, he and his housemates repeated the previous night's antics, meowing in front of the bedroom door. This time, Poppy did not respond.

"He's mad at us," Mandee said, and gave up. Khan watched the door for a while, then retired to his spot on the sofa. For two more nights, they tried the same, but Poppy ignored them. On the third night, Khan stayed upstairs, sleeping beside the door, scared. Phantom joined him at the first light of dawn.

"Why are you here?"

"I'm scared," Khan answered. "I think Momma is not coming back. I think she went to the Big Sleep."

"No!" Phantom recoiled at the notion. "No! Poppy is concerned, yes, but not that upset!"

"He never cries when he's upset like Momma does," Khan said softly. His heart squeezed with grief. "He's never home as much like he used to be. He never went out after work before. Now he does. Comes home late. It's change. Momma is gone!"

"No, it can't be," Phantom protested, but snuggled against Khan. Khan watched the door, and he fell asleep, hoping to see Momma again.

Khan woke, and blinked against the rays of the rising sun, which slanted into the hallway window. He glanced at the closed door. Alarm shot though him.

"Why isn't Poppy getting up?"

Beside him, Phantom jerked awake. Mandee appeared at the top of the steps.

"He should have awakened a while ago."

"We should wake him," Khan said, and rushed the door. He scratched at the bottom, rattling the door in the frame. Mandee joined him, meowing. Phantom added his voice to the ruckus. Poppy opened the door, and smiled down at them.

"You silly cats are too much," he said, and walked downstairs. Khan followed, leading his housemates. Poppy whistled as he entered the bathroom.

"He is in a good mood," Khan said, and sat down. "How can he be? Momma is gone."

"I don't know," Phantom replied, and settled in front of his dish. Khan turned away, and left the room. He sat in the stairwell window, watching the morning progress, his heart heavy. He watched Poppy's car leave, then left the window to curl on the sofa. He ignored Phantom's invitations to wrestle. Phantom finally sat in front of the couch.

"Why won't you play?"

"I just don't feel like it," Khan answered, and covered his nose with his bushy tail. Phantom uttered a soft growling sigh, then left the room. Khan dozed until he heard the sound of Poppy's car returning. He jerked alert, aware of the time -- late morning. Khan ran into the dining room to find Phantom already there.

"Why is Poppy home now?"

The sound of two car doors closing alerted Khan. A tremor of hope shivered his entire body. The front door opened, and, to Khan's utter delight, Poppy entered, accompanied by another. The footfalls sounded slow and unsteady.

"Easy, Hon," Poppy's gentle voice held joy.

"I'm all right," the other answered, and that voice sent Khan's heart pounding with jubilation.

"Momma!" Khan meowed, hurrying into the foyer. Mandee and Phantom followed him.

"Momma?"

Momma walked into the foyer, leaning on a walking stick, and stopped. Khan rubbed against her legs in joyous circles. He barely acknowledged his housemates' delight.

"Momma! Momma! We missed you!" he purred, echoed by Phantom and Mandee. Momma leaned down to stroke each of them. Phantom scented her deeply and purred.

"She smells right now! The sickness is gone!"

Khan sniffed her hands, and agreed with deep purrs.

"Hello, my babies! Were you good kitties while Momma was gone?"

"Ha!" Poppy laughed. "They drove me nuts. Here, Hon, lay here."

Poppy guided her into the livingroom, and helped her to the sofa. She settled on Khan's sleeping spot, but he cared not at all. His heart sang with joy.

"Momma's home! Momma's home!" Mandee meowed, until Poppy let her outside. Khan heard her happy cries as she announced it to the outdoor feline community. Phantom circled once, then hurried to the kitchen. Khan sneezed with feline mirth as the sounds of flying kibble reached his ears. He knew his buddy sat by the bowls, steam-shoveling food into his mouth. Khan jumped on the sofa, and snuggled by Momma's feet. He purred himself to sleep, happy to have her in his sight, scent, and touch.

Momma stirred, and slowly got up, waking Khan. In alarm, Khan leaped to the floor and walked with her, twittering.

"I'll help you, Momma. I'll guide you. I'll protect you," he babbled, accompanying Momma into the bathroom. Poppy chuckled, his voice echoing from the kitchen.

"You have a furball glued to your walking stick."

"I know," Momma laughed, stroking Khan's back. "Isn't it so sweet?"

Khan refused to leave Momma's side, except to eat and use the pottybox. That night, unable to climb the stairs to the bedroom, Momma slept on the sofa. Khan snoozed with her. He lifted his head when Poppy came down in the morning, whistling. He smiled at Khan as he passed. Phantom hurried into the kitchen, his happy meows echoing to Khan's ears. The radio came to life, and Poppy sang along with it. Noises from outside caught Khan's attention. He recognized Mandee's and Black's voices. He glanced at Momma, who slept soundly, then he jumped off the sofa and hurried to the open window. He looked down, and saw Black following Mandee across the grass. Khan smiled in amusement.

"I'm happy for you," Black said. Mandee's reply disappeared under a groan which issued from the livingroom. Khan looked down into the room, and saw Momma struggling to sit up.

"Momma!" he cried, and bounded down the steps, slipping once on the landing, his paws pounding the wood. He dashed into the livingroom, then clawed to a stop at Momma's feet. She gripped her walking stick, trying to get to her feet.

"Momma! I'm sorry I left you!" Khan cried in piteous meows, hooking his tail to one side. He inhaled deeply, taking in her scent, relieved he smelled no sickness or wrongness. Momma looked down at him in surprise, then beamed a smile at him.

"Oh, my sweet teddy bear of a Coon! Momma is all right -- just a bit sore, that's all."

With effort, Momma rose to her feet and shuffled to the bathroom. Khan paced at her side, his heart bursting with love and delight. Khan gazed at her once they reached the bathroom. Color flushed her cheeks again, and her eyes sparkled. Then Khan spied the ugly pink scar on her belly. Alarm flashed through him, but suddenly he knew that something removed the bad sickness from Momma during her absence. Jubilation and relief flooded him. That night, he left Momma's side in the deep dark. He tossed all his anxieties aside, and engaged Phantom in a long overdue bout of wrestling. Though he tried not to think about the last few days, worry that this might happen again drove him to expend all his pent-up energies in his pounces, strikes, and spins.

# CHAPTER 8: CANINE INTRUDER

A suncycle passed swiftly once life returned to normal. One cool afternoon, Khan snoozed in the big cat carrier, snuggled into the soft terry liner. He flicked an ear as the sound of a strange car entering the driveway floated into the window. Momma went outside to greet the visitor. Khan listened to Momma's voice, then opened his eyes, intrigued by the stranger's speech. The jingle of a chain reached his ears, then the front door opened. Momma entered with a strange woman, but Khan forgot the human as the panting and heavy footfalls of a large animal echoed up the foyer. He turned in the carrier, facing out, watching as the visitor led a huge dog into the dining room. The scrabble of claws on flooring reverberated in the house as the rest of his housemates dove for hiding places.

"Hide! Hide!" Mandee's high hiss of warning followed. A flash of fear raced along Khan's nerves, but he ignored it. Who dared enter his territory? Khan listened for his buddy's voice, but Phantom, as always, hid when strangers came to visit.

The enormous black-and-tan dog laid down obediently beside its owner. Khan met eyes with Momma, and saw a touch of concern in her gaze. Khan flicked his ear, and watched the dog; then, after many minutes, he decided not to fear this intruder. He stretched, and walked out of the safe confines of his sleeping place. He settled under one of the dining room chairs, and stared at the dog.

"Who are you?" Khan asked with a growl. The dog glanced at him, cocked its head, and only whined.

"You don't understand catspeak?"

The dog stared at him, but did not move. Khan held the dog's gaze, his amber eyes calm and alert. The dog looked away. All afternoon, while Momma entertained the visitor, Khan eyed the dog. Suddenly, Momma's question caught Khan's attention.

"He seems well-behaved, especially with my Khan mere feet away from him. Does he like cats?"

"Oh, yes, Damien loves cats. I have two," the visiting human said. "They play all the time. He grew up with them."

"That is wonderful," Momma said, laughing. "Seems my Khan must know this. Look. He is out of the carrier."

Khan blinked at Momma as the two women stared at him. He tucked his feet under him, and stared at the dog.

"He is either very brave, or stupid," the visitor giggled.

"Just very brave, and knows his strength," Momma retorted with pride. Khan returned his attention to Damien, and tilted his ears back.

"You play with cats? Yet you don't know our speech?"

"I know catspeak," the dog said, turning to face him.

"Why didn't you answer me before?"

"I thought you were angry. I didn't want to start a fight. My momma would be very mad at me if I hurt you."

"Hurt me?" Khan yawned, then flexed a huge paw. "You may be bigger than I am, but you don't have four sets of these."

"You are a Maine Coon!" Damien yipped, then flattened his ears, and wagged his tail. "I have respect for your kind."

"As you should," Khan replied, rising and settling closer to the dog. He ignored the clicks of a camera as Momma took photographs.

"I do," Damien said. "I like cats. I like to play with your kind. My friends at home are not as large as you are, but one is a Maine Coon, too. Big feet, big claws."

"I think we can be friends." Khan relaxed his features into a feline smile. "But always remember that this is my house."

"I will," Damien said.

Shortly after Damien uttered those words, the visitor led him out of the house. Khan followed them to the door at a cautious walk.

"You're crazy!" came a hiss from behind a livingroom chair. "He'll eat you up!"

"It's OK, Mandee. He isn't going to hurt us."

"You're too trusting," she hissed in retort.

"Maybe not," Phantom replied from the top of the stairs, a thoughtful look on his face. "Running away may be the worst thing to do. It makes them chase us like we chase mice."

"I am fast," Mandee answered, pride in her tone. "I can out-maneuver any dog."

"As can I, but I am growing bigger every moon cycle. I will see what happens next time a dog comes to chase me."

"Run, run," Mandee grumbled, then fell silent.

"Running away is for scared little kittens," Khan said, amused at the conversation. "This is my home, and I won't run and hide, no matter what comes here."

Khan turned back up the hall, heading for the kitchen. He needed a snack after the day's excitement. Phantom followed, and joined him.

Time passed, and Khan forgot about the huge dog, until, one day, in deep winter, the doorbell announced company. Khan raised his head, but did not relinquish his prime snoozing spot. His housemates scattered to hide. Momma opened the door, and welcomed her friend into the foyer. Khan remembered her, and, before he even thought of the dog, Damien bounded into the room, straining at the end of his lead, hauling his human into the livingroom. Damien stretched his long muzzle toward Khan, panting, whining, his eyes gleaming with excitement.

Anger and outrage surged through Khan, on the heels of a short burst of alarm. Khan slanted his ears, rose slowly to his feet, and puffed his hair. He growled warnings, amber eyes blazing.

"This is my home!"

Damien slid to a stop, and ceased pulling at his lead. He lowered his head, sniffing. He whined. "I want to play!"

"You dare barge into my home, and charge me?' Khan hissed, daring Damien to push his nose within claw reach.

"We are friends! Play?"

"Have you no cat manners?" Khan growled, mincing toward the dog, tail lashing. "Never charge us. You should have come in slowly, and walked to me, to greet me."

"Damien!" The dog's owner cried out. "Be nice to the kitty." She hauled back on his lead, pulling him out of Khan's reach. Khan settled on his haunches, but watched, indignant.

"Khan looks like he wants to take a chunk out of Damien's face," Poppy chuckled. "Not a good idea for a showdog."

"I know," Damien's momma replied. "He only wants to play."

"Khan doesn't think so," Momma said.

"Come on inside. Let them both relax."

"Thanks, but I must go," Damien's momma said. "I just wanted to pop in while I was around here to say hello."

"Not even a cup of coffee?" Momma asked.

"No, thanks. Maybe next time."

With that, Damien and his momma left the house. Khan followed the dog to the door, still full of anger. He sat down after Momma closed the door. Phantom emerged from his upstairs hiding spot. He halted at the bottom of the steps.

"You were so angry! I've never seen you like that."

"He startled me, and, for a moment, I did feel afraid, but then, I just got mad at him for doing that. He says he knows catspeak. He should also know some manners."

"He sure did respect you though," Phantom said, and Khan noticed the gleam in his friend's sea-green eyes.

"What are you thinking?" Khan purred suddenly, picking up an aura of mischief from Phantom.

"This may be interesting," Phantom replied. "It may be more fun to stand my ground when a dog comes at me."

"Dangerous!" Mandee exclaimed, coming out from behind a chair.

"For you, perhaps." Phantom twitched his tail. "But I am nearly twice as big as you."

"So?" Mandee stared aghast. "They will snap you up like we do a mouse."

"Have you ever seen a mouse with these?" Phantom raised a paw, then unsheathed his claws. "If I have cover behind me, these will protect me, and teach all dogs a lesson."

"It is dangerous and crazy. You'll be hurt," Mandee warned.

"Perhaps, but not if I can help it." Phantom ended the discussion by trotting up the hall to the kitchen. Khan watched his buddy disappear, then faced Mandee.

"He may have a good strategy there." Khan touched noses with the offended female. "But I can understand your point, too."

Mandee growled inarticulately, and trotted over to Momma. Khan sneezed a feline laugh, then followed Phantom to the kitchen. He wondered how his best friend might put his plan into action.

Leaf Bloom arrived, with a rush of warmth and sunny days. Khan sat in the window one morning, watching his friend patrol his yard. Suddenly, two large canines galloped across the lawn, heading straight for Phantom, Black, Kilkil, and Mandee. Mandee, Black, and Kilkil scattered and dashed away, but Phantom hurried to the big bushes right outside the window, then turned around, facing out, anticipating the oncoming clash. In silence, the two dogs attacked, the hunting gleam in their eyes. Khan puffed up, and hissed, wishing he stood beside his buddy.

Phantom waited, and, as the two shoved their bared fangs at him, he reared up, and lashed out with both well-armed front paws. In swift succession, faster than Khan's eyes followed, Phantom raked his claws deep into the first dog's face, then hit the other dog before Khan blinked. The rustling of the bush, and no other sound, announced the battle. The first dog yelped, then kiyied in dread, as blood welled from its torn face. It whirled, and raced from the yard. The other dog spun around, and fled in the other direction. Momma jumped from her seat at the computer, and ran outside. Khan heard her praise Phantom, astonishment in her voice. She coaxed him inside. Khan leaped from the windowsill, and ran to his buddy.

"That was amazing!"

"It worked," Phantom replied, his tail up and ramrod straight. "No more marauding dogs in my yard!"

"Good job." Khan touched noses with his friend. "But it may not always be so easy. Black is brave, and he runs, too."

"Faugh! Black is like Mandee and my mama. Small and quick. I am bigger and stronger, and I will be careful. If I have my way, no more dogs will invade our territory," Phantom assured him, and sauntered into the kitchen for a snack. Khan stood on the slate in the foyer, listening to Phantom gobble down kibble. He twitched his tail, then hurried to join Phantom at the food bowls. He watched his buddy eat, then noticed that Phantom stood as tall as he did. Phantom's muscles rippled under his short dark fur, and Khan tried to feel reassured with Phantom's increasing size and strength. He returned to his dinner, hoping his best friend never grew too over-confident. Imagining life without Phantom chilled his blood with a stab of deep sorrow.

© Marie J. S. Phillips

# CHAPTER 9: NEW HOUSEMATES

The moon cycles merged into sun cycles as Khan matured into a enormous Maine Coon of seventeen pounds. His buddy Phantom grew into a huge athletic cat of eighteen pounds who patrolled the yard with ever-increasing boldness. He chased all strangers from the yard, using his skill, strength, and brains. True to his word a suncycle before, Phantom learned to battle dogs, and chased them from his yard with relentless cunning. Khan spent many nice days on his harness outdoors, enjoying his friend's antics, even helping him frighten off a dog or two under Momma's watchful eyes. Dogs bolted when charged by two large cats, confusion and fear in their eyes and body language. Black Satin visited often, and even learned to beg food off Momma, who gave in without question. Phantom's mama, Kilkil, continued to boldly enter the house whenever she saw the opportunity, and only Mandee took offense, despite Phantom's pleas to leave Kilkil alone.

Much to Mandee's disgust, Indy, a brown tabby-and-white Maine Coon kitten, arrived during Khan's third year. That hot summer day, Momma and Poppy opened the carrier to reveal a tiny ball of hissing fluff. Khan pushed his head into the carrier, and hailed the newcomer.

"Hello! I am Khan! Welcome to our house."

"Mama!" the kitten wailed, then hissed, huddling in the rear of the carrier. Khan turned away.

"Let's leave him alone."

The ball of fuzz with the enormous tufted ears crept from the carrier, then dashed across the room to huddle under the hutch. He hissed at all of them, even Momma and Poppy. Khan sat down.

"He is not like you were."

"How was I?" Phantom asked.

"Scared, but you never hissed at Momma or Poppy like that. He is going to be trouble," Khan said.

The next day, the kitten followed him into the livingroom, and crept up to him.

"Mama?"

Khan watched, as Indy lay down beside him on the sofa.

"Mama?"

"I'm not your mama," Khan said softly, and sniffed the kitten's head.

"You look like Mama." Indy snuggled against him, and Khan licked his head.

"Maybe he won't be so bad," he commented to Phantom. Phantom flattened his ears, and lashed his tail.

"He just thinks you're his mother. He'll be trouble. You said it yesterday. I agree."

Much to Khan's disappointment, as Indy grew up, he stopped snuggling up to Khan for comfort. As Indy matured, he developed an aversion to being touched, though he allowed a simple paw tap in simple games of tag. To Khan's dismay, Indy's neurotic dislike of physical contact turned to paranoia. To further his reputation as a psycho cat, Indy talked to his toys, the walls, thin air, and nothing in particular. He enjoyed dropping his toys into the toilet and water bowls. Much to Khan's disgust, Indy loved to slosh the bowl until water spilled all over the floor.

"Why must you mess the water bowl up?" he growled at Indy one morning. Indy turned a mischievous face to him, shaking his pristine white paws.

"It's so much fun!"

"Fun? It's fun to get your feet all wet? Yeeuck!" Khan subconsciously shook each foot.

"Fun, my big butt," Phantom growled, mincing through a puddle to get to his food. "Momma is gonna be angry with you."

"So? It's fun," Indy hissed in retort, and darted from the room.

"He is crazy," Phantom mumbled as he ate.

"Momma gets mad at him a lot, too," Khan remarked, and ate breakfast.

Another suncycle passed with few incidents, but during Khan's fourth year, young Maine Coon kitten Warlocke arrived on a cool evening in late No Leaf. Smokey-black with a white undercoat, the fuzzy kitten ran and hid from everyone.

"I hope he isn't going to be like Indy," Phantom grumbled.

"He may not. He didn't hiss," Khan said, and followed little Warlocke around.

"Hi! I'm Khan! Welcome. Don't be scared!" Warlocke paused, and gazed up at Khan. Khan sat down, and lowered his head to sniff the kitten.

"Big, like my mama," the ball of black fluff mewled.

"Oh, a kitten!" Indy said, coming downstairs.

"Don't scare him," Phantom warned.

"I'm gonna play with him," Indy said, and charged the kitten. Warlocke squealed in alarm, bringing Momma and Poppy into the room. They scolded Indy for hurting the new baby.

"You idiot," Khan growled. "You play too rough."

"I'll try to be gentle," Indy said.

"Don't try, DO be gentle," Khan retorted, glaring at Indy, bushy tail twitching to and fro. Indy turned away, and ran up to Warlocke, tapped him playfully, then ran away. Little Warlocke watched, and a mischievous gleam entered his green eyes.

"Play!" he mewed in a high-pitched voice, and ran after Indy. In minutes, the two engaged in an energetic game of tag, pleasing Momma and Poppy. Khan relaxed, and purred dep approval.

"Well, he is doing something right for a change. As for me, I'll not play with a silly kitten," Mandee growled, watching from a chair.

Unlike Indy, Warlocke grew up sweet, gentle, and fun. His fuzzy black coat grew long and silky, touched with the silver highlights characteristic of black smoke coloring. Khan and Phantom welcomed him into their play sessions, unable to comprehend Indy's "Don't

Touch Me" attitude. Indy wailed and hissed whenever Warlocke tried to wrestle him. The young Maine Coon joined Khan and Phantom with delight, but loved antagonizing Indy during their sessions of tag.

"Why do you pounce on him when you know he hates it?" Khan asked one day.

"He's all noise and bluster," Warlocke answered merrily. "I can whip his butt, and he knows it."

"But you put him in such a snit, that he's impossible to get along with," Phantom said, flashing his fangs.

"He'll get over it." Warlocke purred, thoroughly amused. Khan flicked his ears, noting the mischief gleaming in Warlocke's eyes.

"He may, but you make him so upset," Khan commented. "He snarls every time he sees you after you pounce on him."

"I don't care," Warlocke laughed. "It's funny. He can't dominate me anymore, and it drives him crazy."

"We know," Khan responded, flattening his ears. "If you don't care that he hisses at you all the time, then I don't either."

Warlocke merely purred, and sauntered out of the room.

As Leaf Bloom turned to Full Leaf, a short-legged stray entered the yard, begging for food, braving Black's, Kilkil's, and Phantom's anger. Mandee ignored him. Khan liked the little cat.

"Remember what it was like to be hungry?" Khan admonished his feline friends one day as he lounged in the grass, wearing his red harness. The cats sat in the shade of the old Norway Spruce Momma called Old Gent. Black grumbled, but capitulated, refraining from attacking the newcomer, who walked to the back porch where a bowl of food sat out for him. Kilkil wrinkled her pretty orange-and-grey face into a scowl.

"He's not coming to MY house! We already have too many!" she snarled, then stalked off, hurrying home before Mandee decided to attack her. Phantom turned his head away, but his purr told Khan his buddy held no anger.

Full Leaf waxed warm and delightful. Khan enjoyed many days outdoors, getting to know the strange short-legged cat. The others teased him, calling him all sorts of names like woodchuck, stubby, and rodent brain . One late Full Leaf day, Khan enjoyed the sunny afternoon. The newcomer approached him and Momma, ignoring the other cats. Phantom and Mandee stared at him from the back walkway.

"Why won't you go find another home, Stubby." Mandee hissed.

"I like it here," the short-legged cat answered serenely, and sat on the grass beside Momma's lounger. "My name is Munchkin."

"Don't be so pompous," Phantom warned, then sneezed a feline laugh. "You stay even after Momma made you go get shots."

"And neutered you," Black grumbled.

"Your momma and poppy neutered you, too, Black." Khan said, eyeing his old friend. "I don't see you running away."

"We have enough cats around here," Mandee growled. Black snorted, and trotted after Kilkil.

"Don't listen to them," Khan told the newcomer. "Momma likes you. So do I. But I am sorry she took you to the cat doctor. I hope it didn't hurt you too much."

"Thank you," the young cat purred. "It was scary, but once I healed I felt fine. I only wish I could come inside with you, but I know Phantom dislikes me."

"He is just territorial. He won't hurt you if I say so." Khan said with confidence, glancing at his buddy, who washed his feet. "Besides he chases dogs away that go after you, too. If he really hated you he wouldn't do that." Khan purred, sensing the five cat household already numbered six, even if Phantom. Mandee, and Indy did not realize it yet.

As Full Leaf turned to Leaf Fall, and cold breezes chilled the nights, Khan's momma picked up the short-legged cat and his bowls, and carried him inside one chilly afternoon.

"Now, you guys be nice to Munchkin," she said sternly to Khan's housemates, as she set him and his food bowl on the floor. She stroked Khan's head and smiled. "I know you will be good to him. You're such a good boy."

Munchkin leaped and scrambled to the sink, to peer down at Khan and his housemates. Khan gazed up at him, tail raised in friendly greeting.

"You shouldn't be afraid. You know us. We only want to play."

"I know that, you know that, but do they?" Munchkin meowed in his screaky voice.

"Don't ever touch me," Indy growled, but eyed the newcomer with mischief in his big green eyes.

"Be quiet," Khan snarled at the temperamental Maine Coon in uncharacteristic anger. Indy mumbled, and returned his attention to Munchkin. Nobody moved. After a few hours, Khan stood up.

"Come on, let him eat." He swatted playfully at Phantom. "Why are you so upset if he eats some food? Momma always refills the bowls."

"I like you," Warlocke said to Munchkin. "I won't ever hurt you."

"You like me?" Munchkin replied, his soft raspy voice full of surprise. "Everyone hates me."

"I don't," Warlocke purred.

"Look at him," Phantom sneezed in mirth. "He looks like a woodchuck with those short legs!"

"I like him," Warlocke said. "Stop being so mean."

"So do I," Khan agreed. "Come on, let him be."

"All right." Phantom rose, then stretched. "You win. He eats."

Khan led his buddy out of the room, blinking a feline smile, when he heard a thud in the kitchen. Munchkin jumped off the sink to enjoy a meal. From that day on, Munchkin endeared himself to the entire family, human and feline alike. Phantom's teasing continued, but he never attacked or hurt Munchkin. Mandee tolerated him well, only smacking him on the head occasionally to remind him she remained queen of this home. Khan loved his big happy family.

One morning, Warlocke and Indy played tag, the same game they played the night of Warlocke's arrival. Warlocke chased Indy into the kitchen, and pounced on him. Indy snarled in fury.

"Don't touch me!"

"But I want to wrestle," Warlocke retorted, tail lashing, legs trembling. Khan sat by the litter box, and twitched his tail in amusement.

"He will never change," Khan purred. Phantom looked up from his food bowl.

"Why do you bother?"

"It's fun," Warlocke answered, his long silver-touched black-smoke fur bristling with indignation. Munchkin watched with amusement from his perch on dining room chair.

"But he even hates Momma to touch him and groom him. Proves he's crazy," Phantom growled, and returned to eating.

"I can't help it," Indy wailed, and ran from the room. Phantom uttered a growl. and returned to his breakfast. Warlocke trotted into the next room, and started his own game with his favorite catnip doll. Momma called it Warlocke's Billy Boy toy. Khan wondered what that meant, but only gleaned the toy portrayed a famous human. Khan forgot the toy and trotted up to Phantom, tapping his butt with a big paw.

"Come on, glutton! Catch me if you can!"

Khan whirled, and ran from the room on thunderous paws. Phantom left his food, and followed.

"You know I can catch you! I'm fast. I'm strong," cried Phantom, as he caught up to Khan. Khan gleefully turned to meet him, and they wrestled in joy on the livingroom rug. Phantom sat up suddenly, pulling free of Khan's embrace.

"What?"

Khan asked, paws up in the air.

"You have lost some weight. Are you eating?"

"Yes, of course I am!" Khan rolled over, and regarded Phantom. "I always lose weight, but I put it back on."

"I hope so," Phantom trotted out of the room. "Come on! Prove it, and eat!"

Khan rose, and followed his buddy to the food bowls, forced by his body to detour to the litterbox. He completed his business, sauntered to the bowls, then ate, wondering why his best pal worried so much about a bit of weight loss.

## CHAPTER 10: THE TESTS

The moon cycles merged into a quiet happy life, until one morning in Full Leaf, Momma picked Khan up and remarked, "You are getting so thin."

Khan uttered a growling purr as she set him in front of the food bowls.

"Eat!"

Khan dutifully chewed his kibble. Phantom settled beside him.

"You are thin now," he remarked. "Told you so."

Khan growled, knowing Momma planned to take him to the cat doctor again.

"You never put the weight back on," Phantom said between mouthfuls.

"But I eat," Khan protested.

"But having the watery poop is bad," Phantom reminded him.

"I know, and it does upset my belly," Khan admitted.

Later that morning, Phantom watched, as Momma packed Khan into the carrier.

"No, Momma, I don't want to go!" Khan protested with a bleat, but he let her push him im nto the crate. Khan settled onto the soft towel, heart pounding. No matter how he told himself not to be afraid, his fear rose, and his heart thudded inside his ribcage.

At the Animal Hospital, the doctor examined Khan, then sent him home with medications, but Khan still suffered from what his momma called "the bad doodies." Over the next moon cycle, trips to the cat doctor increased, and Khan hated the poking, the prodding, and all the testing.

One afternoon, during yet another visit to the cat doctor, a nurse took him in back. He heard Momma and the doctor conversing in worried voices. A nurse placed him in a cage, and Khan waited, full of anxiety. The doctor soon returned, and took him from his cage, then laid him on a cold metal table. Khan wiggled to free himself, uttering his bobcat bellow.

"Stay still, Big Guy," the doctor said soothingly. "We only need some x-rays."

"X-rays?" he howled his query. They held him down, maneuvering a large machine above his body. He fought, fear taking over his entire being. The doctor stood up.

"Let him up. We aren't going to get good shots tonight. He is too panicky. Put him in his cage for the evening. I'll tell his owner he must stay the night. Tomorrow, we'll sedate him a bit, and try again."

The cat nurse returned Khan to his cage. Khan huddled on the bedding, eyes wide with dread. His heart raced, and he breathed heavily. He never before stayed away from home overnight, and recalled his shelter days with rising terror. As the hospital darkened and quieted, Khan mewled with fear.

"Momma! Momma! Why leave me here?"

"The doctors will take good care of you." A feline voice purred out of the dark. A grey-brown tabby cat materialized out of the gloom, and leaped up onto the exam table near Khan's cage. "Greetings. I am Oliver."

"Oliver?" Khan jerked his head around, bristling, but his innate friendliness stopped any further aggression. Khan stood up, and pushed his nose against the cage bars. "Greetings. I'm Khan. I've seen you out front. Why are you here?"

"I live here." Oliver blinked a reassuring feline smile at Khan. "Don't worry so much. It's always scary the first time you must stay overnight in the hospital. You'll be fine."

"How do you know?"

"I see much here," Oliver replied, then abruptly jumped down when another cat in a cage across the room began to hiss and snarl insults. "I have to leave. The doc doesn't like it when I upset other cats, but you are a very nice cat. Try not to be so scared."

"I'll try. Thanks." Khan watched the tabby amble out of the room, then laid his head down. He took comfort in Oliver's confident words, and fell asleep. In the morning, he woke with a start. Confusion clouded his mind, until he remembered the previous day's events. He waited as the cat nurses and doctor arrived, and, soon, they came to his cage. One nurse injected him with a needle, and he felt relaxed in moments. Khan laid on the table, wiggling occasionally, allowing the nurses to stretch him out as the doctor took the x-rays needed to help him. When the doctor finished the tests, a cat nurse returned Khan to his cage. He waited, and, as the drug wore off, his fears of never going back home returned to him. As the day waxed, the room brightened with sunlight, and a cat nurse cheerfully hailed him.

"Time to go, Big Guy," she said, and took him out of the cage. She carried Khan out to the reception area, where he spotted his momma. Joy coursed through Khan as Momma hugged him, then placed him in the familiar carrier. He listened as Momma spoke with the doctor, and felt his joy fade.

"He needs a sonogram," the doctor said. "His heart looked enlarged on the x-ray. Take him to this

Animal Hospital. They have a wonderful cardiologist there."

Days later, Momma took him on a long journey to a strange cat doctor. He huddled in the carrier, sensing his momma's fears. Finally, the doctor brought him in, setting him on a cold steel table. The doctor ran his hands over Khan while talking, and Khan heard strange words like hyperthyroid. His heart pounded with terror, and he cried as Momma left the exam room.

"Mommaaaaa!" he wailed. The strange doctor shaved Khan's chest and sides. The noise of the machine poured adrenaline into Khan's body. He struggled against the doctor and the doctor's assistants. They held him down, running a weird contraption over the shaved areas. Khan bellowed his wildcat cry of fear, ignoring the image on the screen near the table. After they took away the machine, they stuck a needle into him, drawing blood. He cried, wanting to go home, wanting to shut this strange place from his senses.

Finally, like a gift from the ancient cat gods, his momma walked in the door. Khan's pounding heart slowed, as hope sprouted.

"Go home?" he queried her in his soft meow.

"He has the biggest thyroid I've ever felt," the doctor told Momma. "It is odd for so young a cat. But we will know for sure when his test comes back. As for his heart, it is slightly enlarged, but healthy. "

"Thank you, Doctor," Momma said, as she lifted Khan's carrier. She opened the door, and he darted inside that safe familiar haven. Khan sensed her relief, but undercurrent worry remained. He did not understand what under the sun these doctors searched for, but Momma fussed over his gaunt frame. To his delight, Momma did take him home, but the trips continued, to his normal doctor, who poked him with needles and took blood. He huddled on the exam table as his doctor examined his neck.

"I do not understand," Khan's doctor commented. "I feel only his thick neck muscles. His thyroid feels fine. But we can take the Free T-4 test."

"Yes," Momma agreed, and the doctor took more blood from Khan, who felt as if millions of cats pierced him with their claws.

"We will put him on a medication to help the diarrhea, but he may have a food intolerance and allergy. It may take a while to figure it out."

"I will do whatever is necessary," Momma replied, and Khan cringed. What do they mean? Once home, Khan hid upstairs. Each trip to the doctor for his weigh-ins fueled his growing fears, and he withdrew from household activities. Terror took over his life. Momma cried over him when his appetite vanished. One afternoon, he sat huddled on the library sofa, when Phantom walked into the room.

"Why are you hiding?"

"Scared," Khan mewled like a kitten. "I don't want to go to the doctor anymore."

"But they need to find out what is wrong." Phantom sat down. "Momma is very upset that you aren't eating."

"I can't. My tummy hurts," Khan wailed. "The medicine tastes so bad I want to throw up! I drool and drool, and it foams! I feel like an insane cat with a bad disease."

"You must eat," Phantom growled in annoyance. "Momma says they can't find what is wrong. You are making her cry. Poppy is upset, too. That medicine took away the bad poops, right?"

"Yes."

"Then eat!" Phantom snarled, and stalked from the room.

The next morning, Momma came into the room and scooped him up. She gave him to Poppy, who held him firmly. Khan tensed, knowing Momma planned to give him a nasty pill.

"Noo!" he mewled, and tried to struggle. Poppy grasped him tightly, and Momma popped the pill down his throat. Khan raced back upstairs to hunker on the sofa. He licked his lips, expecting that horrible bitter flavor, but he tasted nothing. The minutes passed, and Khan felt his entire body relax. His belly rumbled with sudden hunger. He jumped from the sofa, almost tripped over his own paws, and lumbered down the stairs. He hurried straight to his bowl and munched down the kibble. He heard Momma exclaim in pure delight.

"He's eating! He's eating!"

Khan purred, and enjoyed the food.

"Whatever was in that pill made you eat like me!" Phantom remarked, taking a place at one of the bowls heaped with kibble.

"I feel good," Khan mumbled. "I don't feel scared any more."

A few days later, while chowing down a nice dinner, Khan heard Momma tell Poppy something about a food intolerance, and wonderful news that he did not have something called hyperthyroidism. Khan understood little of what she said, but gleaned that one of the foods in the dry kibble mix caused his bad doodies. From that day, Khan ate well, put on weight, and, after a shot from the cat doctor, his occasional bad doodies went away. His fears diminished, as did his trips to the doctor. Life again went well, until Leaf Bloom.

On a cool, sunny afternoon, Phantom rushed in the door when Momma responded to his strident cries. Khan noticed Momma seemed a little upset as well.

"What is wrong?"

"Black's momma left and took my mama and sisters away!"

"What?" Khan bristled from nose to tail tip.

"She and another human put them into carriers and drove away! I saw them take Mama! She screamed for me! So did my sisters! I couldn't help them! Old Oreo, and Peanut, and Squeakers are gone too!"

"What about Black??" Khan mewled.

"I don't know! I didn't see him, or Rumple, but Bobo ran across the street. He hid in the neighbor's garage!"

"I must go outside!!!" Khan meowed in his bathtime bellow, but did not get the opportunity until

Momma harnessed him up one warm morning days later. He pulled at the harness, dragging Momma out with all his strength. He reached the center of the back yard, and stopped, facing into the breeze. Momma put the metal stake in the ground and tied Khan's long lead to it. She left to work in the gardens. Above him, the old Spruce that shaded the yard sang softly, but Khan ignored the enticing sound.

"Black! BLACK!" he called. Only Old Gent's song and rustling grasses met his plea. He raised his voice to a bobcat wail. "BLACK!"

"I think he's gone too," Phantom said softly.

"I have not seen him, either." Mandee added, and sat in the sun. "I hope he was not taken."

"No! No!" Khan wailed, straining against the harness, wanting to rush into the bushes at the property's edge, Black's favorite haunt. Suddenly, a familiar shape materialized out of the shadows of the bushes.

Black sauntered out onto the sunny lawn, and Khan's heart swelled with joy and relief.

"Black!"

"Hey, Khan! What is it that has you bellowing?" Black stopped in front of Khan.

"I am soo glad to see you! Phantom said your momma left and took his mama and sisters and the rest with her! I thought you went with them." Khan's tail drooped. "I thought you were gone forever."

"No, I am here. I escaped the roundup."

"Roundup?" Khan and Phantom responded in unison. Black sneezed his mirth.

"Yes, my momma and poppy had problems, and she left. I don't understand it all, but your mama and most of them went away with her. I was on my way home to grab lunch when I heard Kilkil screaming and wailing. I hid and listened, and did not come out even when they called my name. I peeked out around the house and saw all my housemates in carriers in a strange car. Bobo ran across the street. Only Rumple remained free, and nobody seemed to care. I think our Poppa refused to let them take Rumple. I bolted and hid down there in the brush for days." Black paused, his eyes wide. "I think they meant to take me, too, but, no matter what happens, even if I had to live outside all the time, I never want to leave this place."

"I don't want you to leave, ever," Khan said and touched Black's nose.

Later that night, in the quiet house, Khan reflected on the day's events, and his recent trips to the cat doctor. He worried that it might all happen again.

# CHAPTER 11: SHATTERED JAW

A few suncycles passed, and an accident broke the happy chaos of Khan's life. Late one night, Khan and Phantom raced up and down the polished wood stairs, romping in glee. The speakers of Poppy's stereo system boomed with the sounds of a movie, drowning out the noise Khan and Phantom produced with their wrestling.

"Can't catch me!" Phantom trilled, racing back up the steps. Khan leaped after his pal, catching him at the top of the stairs. He pounced on Phantom's rear, and Phantom spun around to meet him, eyes full of mischief. Suddenly, Phantom's feet slipped on the narrow curved steps, and he fell. Khan cried out, and Phantom let out a startled meow. Phantom's lower jaw struck the edge of the step, and a sharp crack reverberated in Khan's ears, followed by a howl of pain from his buddy. Blood from the mangled bone dripped to the steps. Khan stared, eyes widening, while Phantom scrabbled to regain his footing, and the ruckus attracted attention from Momma, who shouted above the movie.

"Take it easy, guys! Don't play so rough!"

Phantom scrambled back up the stairs to huddle on the rug.

"Oh! Oh! It hurts!" Phantom cried. Khan stared at his friend, aghast. Phantom's lower jaw hung from his head, twisted and bleeding. His eyes dilated with the agony. Khan felt pain radiating from his buddy in waves.

"Go show Momma! Now! You are hurt!"

"Can't move! OH! OW! OWWW!" Phantom panted. Khan sat beside him, not knowing what to do. The house matriarch, Mandee, ascended the stairs, followed by young Warlocke. Indy peered out of the library. Munchkin watched from the bottom of the stairs.

"He is right," Mandee growled at him. "It is bad."

"Horrible!" Indy cried, eyes wide, and he vanished back into the library.

"You're a big help," Mandee snarled at him. "Coward."

"Tell Momma," Warlocke said, his green eyes wide and bright in his black mask.

"You must tell Momma," Munchkin added. "I always let Momma know when I feel ill."

"I am not peeing on a towel or in Poppy's shoes," Phantom gasped, his breath ragged. "That is the wrong way to do it."

"It's the only way I know how," Munchkin mewed, and fell quiet.

Finally, Phantom's breathing slowed, and he gazed at Khan with wide but more normal eyes.

"It feels better now."

"Go show Momma! It's bad!" Khan insisted. "You only think you feel better."

"Your body is shocked," Mandee said with a hiss. "It's trying to numb the pain."

"All right." Phantom rose to his feet, and descended the steps on the wall side, giving the narrow turn a wide berth. With a shake, he continued down the stairs, and sauntered into the livingroom, straight to Momma. Khan followed, glancing down at the stairs. Drops of blood splattered the polished wood, and Khan carefully avoided them. The scent of Phantom's blood twitched his nostrils. He halted mid-stairwell, and watched through the railing.

"Phantom? What do you have in your mouth?" Momma asked him, sitting up. "Oh, my God! Phantom, what have you done? Honey! Look at what Phantom did!"

Momma scooped Phantom up, and knelt in front of Poppy. In a flurry of activity, they whisked Phantom into the kitchen. Khan listened to the talk.

"Yep, he broke his jaw," Poppy said.

"What do we do? It's one-thirty in the morning," Momma wailed in panic. Khan walked into the kitchen, where Phantom lay on the floor.

"They picked up the food on me," Phantom complained.

"You tried to eat?" Khan stared aghast.

"Yes. I'm hungry."

Khan lifted his head, alert to the fear in Momma's voice as she and Poppy spoke. Momma wanted to take him to a cat doctor, far away. Khan remembered the strange cat doctor he saw not so long ago, and he bristled. He turned, and ran up the stairs, scared by his own fear. He huddled at the top of the steps, ears quivering, and relaxed when Poppy's reason won over Momma's panic.

"Look, Hon, he tried to eat. He's not in dire pain. It's only a few hours until morning."

"I know, but LOOK at him!"

"Hon, it's raining outside, and the emergency clinic is a good half-hour drive, longer in this weather. How many animals will be there waiting to be seen? In this weather, I am sure there will be many. Look, he's doing OK. We can wait the few hours until morning, and let him see his own doctor."

That night, Khan slept near his buddy, aware of Momma's checking on Phantom often during the remainder of the night. The next morning, Momma and Poppy took Phantom to the cat doctor. Khan waited, nervous and upset. When they returned without his friend, he cuddled on Momma's feet.

"Where is he?"

Momma picked him up, and hugged him.

"It's all right, my big bear."

"But where is he?" Khan meowed. Momma did not understand. Two days passed, and, finally, Phantom returned home. Khan ran up to him as he walked out of the carrier.

"Are you all right?"

"Yes." Phantom hurried straight for the kitchen and the food bowls.

"Is food all you think about?" Khan said in exasperation. 'What did they do?"

"I don't know, really, except that they put my jaw back together."

Khan looked, and, sure enough, Phantom's lower jaw looked normal, except for the glint of metal as he moved.

"Does it hurt?"

"Not real bad," Phantom flashed him a feline smile, blinking his eyes. "I am so glad to be home. I thought Momma and Poppy left me there."

"I am glad they didn't." Khan rubbed his buddy's face gently. "I don't think they would have anyway."

"I didn't either, until night came. They never left me there at night before. I was scared."

"I was worried, too," Khan admitted. "You looked so hurt."

"It hurt a lot, but they fixed me up. I still don't like going there. I hate the needles and all that, but I'm glad Poppy talked Momma into waiting to see our doc and not some strange doctor." Phantom stood up. "Met a cat who lives at the hospital. His name is Oliver. Did you meet him in all your trips there?"

"Yes. I like Oliver. He reminds me of Black in many ways."

"He's not like Black. Black isn't as wise."

"Yes, he is," Khan retorted. "If you took the time to talk to him, and not chase and fight him, you'd learn that. I bet if you weren't caged you'd have tried to fight Oliver, too."

"I wouldn't have," Phantom objected, and headed down the foyer. Khan followed.

"Maybe not there, but what if he walked into our yard?"

"Well," Phantom paused at the livingroom threshold. "Maybe."

"You would have," Khan growled. "I know you. I really wish you'd get to know Black, and not be so jealous."

"I'm not jealous," Phantom hissed in rebuttal.

"Yes, you are. Ever since they took your mama away and you saw that Black escaped and she didn't, you fight with him more. I wish you wouldn't be so upset."

"I'm sorry. I can't help it sometimes. You're my best friend in all the world." Phantom shuffled into the room. "I still miss my mama. I wish she had escaped like he did."

"And you are mine. I wish Kilkil had escaped. I miss her, too." Khan said, following Phantom into the livingroom. Phantom jumped onto his favorite chair, and curled up.

Khan jumped up onto the cushion with him.

"Tired?"

"Yes, I need a nap." Phantom groomed Khan's ear. "Black does get an attitude sometimes that I can't stand. Let's not argue about him, OK?"

"Agreed. I still don't understand why any of you get so angry at each other on sight sometimes." Khan nuzzled Phantom's cheek.

"You are the odd one," Phantom blinked his eyes in amusement. "Your oblivious overtures to strangers baffles us all."

"I can't help it. I like everyone. I'll stay here with you. I need a nap, too." Khan curled up beside his friend, but, unlike Phantom, who soon fell fast asleep, Khan lay awake, watching the night pass. Only when the lights went out, after Momma and Poppy retired to bed, did Khan finally fall into slumber.

To Khan's delight, Phantom's jaw healed quickly, though while the metal held his jaw together, Phantom did not want to wrestle and romp. Khan understood. In a mere moon cycle, the cat doctor removed the metal from Khan's buddy's jaw. From that point, in their play, Khan never ran up the narrow part of the stairs, and Phantom avoided the area, giving it a wide berth. The scent of blood lingered a long time, even after Momma cleaned all visible stains away.

## CHAPTER 12: GRIEF

A sun cycle after Phantom's accident, Mandee fell ill. She refused to eat, and vomited every time she tried to drink water, which she did very often. She kept to herself, and visited the cat doctor many times. One night, after lights out, Khan sat in the livingroom with Phantom. Mandee hid behind one of the chairs, behaving so unlike herself that Khan worried about her.

"Leave me alone!" she hissed at Indy, who peeked behind the chair.

"She smells wrong," Khan lamented to Phantom, then turned an angry glare at Indy. "Why do you harass her? You are making her hide!"

"I can't help it," Indy grumbled, and left the room.

"He is crazy," Khan growled. "He bothers Munchkin when he feels ill, now he's bothering Mandee? Why?"

"I am not sure," Phantom answered. "But he's not wrong, really. It seems right to chase away sick cats, but Momma hates when we do that, so I don't."

One day, Mandee did not return home from the cat doctor. For many days, Momma cried and cried. Khan knew Mandee went to the Big Sleep. A few days later, Momma brought home a small green tin, and taped a tiny photo of Mandee to it.

"My poor little Mandee-Mau,"Momma sobbed, and put the tin behind glass in the cabinet. "Rest in peace, sweet one."

Later than day, Momma walked up to Khan while he relaxed on the sofa. Khan stood up.

"Would you like to go outside?" she asked, and, going to the hutch, pulled out Khan's harness. Khan followed, and waited while she buckled the straps, then followed her outside, unsettled and confused. Khan called to Black, hoping to see his friend on this sad occasion. Black Satin materialized, trotting up the lawn.

"What has upset you?"

"I think Mandee went to the Big Sleep!"

"I am not surprised," Black said solemnly. "She was very sick."

"The cat doctor makes sick cats go to the Big Sleep?" Khan asked, appalled.

"Only if they are dying anyway," Black said softly. "It isn't the same as the shelter we were in. Do you think your momma would let them do that if Mandee had any chance to recover?"

"No," Khan replied, twitching his long tail. "She cries a lot. And talked to a small tin box that she brought home today. She says Mandee is there. But I can't scent her. How can she be there?"

"She is, in a way. I don't completely understand it, but the cat doctors put cats who have gone to the Big Sleep into them."

"How do you know that?"

"I learned it from another cat, who lived with cat doctors. I hung around with him before coming here, until someone tried to put out a trap. I left."

Khan glanced down the lawn at bright yellow flowers that stood stark against the brush surrounding them.

"But -- Momma used to cry where those flowers are. Said Demon was there. He lived here before me. I don't understand."

"He was buried there, and not put in fire."

"Fire?" Khan meowed in alarm, bringing Phantom to his side.

"What are you talking about?" Phantom growled.

"Mandee, and the one under those flowers," Black answered, deferring to Phantom, yet not running away.

"Oh," Phantom said softly, and rubbed his cheek on Khan's.

"Is it true? Mandee went in the fire after the Big Sleep?" Khan wailed.

"Yes," Phantom flattened his ears. "She, or what is left of her, is in that tin Momma cries over."

"I don't understand," Khan cried. "Did it hurt her?"

"No," Black responded. "Remember? After the Big Sleep, you can't feel, see, hear, or scent anything ever again."

"Yes, I remember." Khan sat down, mulling over the information. He glanced at the yellow spring flowers. "Why is he there?"

"I don't know, but some mommas bury their cats in the ground. I saw the people on the other side of my house do it last sun cycle."

"I saw that," Phantom whispered. "I was scared. The momma was crying."

"I saw, too," Munchkin said, as he joined the group. "It was so sad."

"Mandee never told you about Demon?" Black asked.

"No. She always said we could never replace him, and never talked about him." Khan narrowed his eyes. "Did she tell you?"

"Yes, she did. We were friends. If she were an intact queen -- ah, oh well." A dreamy look passed over Black's face, before he frowned. "Even after neutering, some of us never forget the attraction of a pretty female.

Anyway, she told me Demon went to the Big Sleep after a terrible accident hurt him bad. His momma -- your momma, that is -- found him already gone. She and your Poppy buried him there. Human mommas do funny things to honor their cat children, which we are," Black said quietly.

"I remember Momma crying when I arrived," Khan mewed. "His scent still was in the house."

"Yes, he went to the Big Sleep two weeks after Phantom and his sisters were born," Black said. "Makes sense that his scent might still be there."

"Oh!" Khan exclaimed, recalling a conversation with his best friend many years ago. He glanced back at Phantom. "Do you remember what you told me the night you came to stay with us for good?"

"What did I say?" Phantom queried.

"That you always knew Momma? That someone told you in your head she was your momma?"

"Yes," Phantom answered, his sea-green eyes thoughtful. "I always felt like that. Why do you ask?"

"Black?" Khan turned to his friend. "Can a cat somehow escape the Big Sleep?"

"Not usually," Black answered. "I am not sure what happens after that. What are you trying to ask me?"

"Well, could Demon have somehow talked to Phantom before he died? Or right after? How else would Phantom know Momma was his, if Demon did not somehow tell him so?"

"Ah, you get into cat spirits and all that. Life essences." Black tilted his head. "All life is recycled. That is true of life energy. What you speak of, I think, is very rare. I am not even sure it can happen."

"Then why did Phantom not fear Momma at all when he first came to us? But he feared me? I think it was Demon. Demon never knew me, but loved Momma and Poppy."

"You know," Phantom interjected, "I sometimes remember things and dream of things I know I could never have seen or done."

"Like what?" Khan asked.

"Like having a long very bushy black tail!" Phantom uttered a sudden snort. "Playing, no, wrestling with Mandee, like you and I play!"

Khan and Black stared at him, aghast. Black slowly twitched his tail.

"Perhaps his spirit joined yours the day he passed. Maybe, maybe, such is possible." Black stood up. "But I have never heard of this before. After the Big Sleep, you scent, see, hear, and feel nothing. That is what I know."

"What if you are wrong?" Khan asked.

"In that case, I can only hope that all of us end up back here, if indeed our life essence cycles after the Big Sleep. But I still think even if our life energy recycles, we remember nothing of it once we are born into new kittens."

Momma suddenly picked Khan up, shattering the conversation. Khan glanced down at Black.

"Thank you, my friend. This has been very intriguing."

Black waved his tail in acknowledgment as he headed to his home.

Khan mused on what he learned. He then decided if he ever went to the Big Sleep, he wanted to be put in a little box in the house, and not buried in the ground. He also hoped that memories of his old life followed him to the next, and, somehow, Momma would find him again. The idea of going to the Big Sleep and leaving Momma upset him, so he never asked Phantom again about those early days. He forced the memories and thoughts to the back of his mind.

That night, after Momma and Poppy retired to bed, Khan wrestled with Phantom on the livingroom rug. They rolled and pounced, thoroughly enjoying themselves, until a soft sizzle in the air stopped the play. Khan lay on his back, stretching his head toward the sound.

"What was that?" Phantom asked, sitting up.

"I don't know," Khan answered, rolling over on his stomach. The crackle sounded again, soft, but a tiny spark of light drew Khan's attention.

"Look!" Khan stared in awe at the cabinet housing Poppy's stereo equipment. Behind the glass, on the bottom shelf, Mandee's new small green tin glowed. The white and pink flowers decorating the box glowed bright, casting shadows across the rug and into the cabinet.

"What is happening?" Phantom crouched, bristling with alarm.

"It's scary!" Indy cried, and Khan glanced backward, spying Indy's face peeking from behind the chair. At that moment, Warlocke hurried into the room.

"I heard a strange noise," he said, and halted, gazing at the glowing tin. Munchkin rolled over in his bed, waking with a snort.

"Why all the fuss? I am trying to sleep."

"Mandee's tin is glowing," Khan replied. Before Khan spoke another word, the glow flared, and a tinkle like breaking glass filled the air. The light condensed into an intense white ball, which floated through the glass to settle on the rug. Iridescent colors swirled through the blinding sphere, and a lone figure materialized in the middle of the light. Tiny bright stars flashed, as the ball formed a halo around the feline form. The figure solidified, and Khan sat up, eyes widening with disbelief.

"Mandee!" he cried, echoed by all his housemates.

Mandee faced them, pinpoint lights dancing over her blue-creme tortoiseshell fur. Bright stars blazed in her green eyes. She purred a greeting.

"Khan, Phantom, Warlocke, Munchkin, and even you, Indy." She slanted her ears back briefly. "Well-met, my old friends."

"It is you! How? Why?" Khan asked in astonishment. "Black says one cannot see, hear, or feel anything after the Big Sleep, even if life energy recycles!"

"He is right, for the most part," Mandee answered, blinking her eyes in a chuckle. "But I defied The Rift. I stayed with my body. I knew if I did, I'd see Momma again."

"The Rift? What is that?" Phantom asked.

"How did you know you'd see Momma again?" Khan added.

"The Rift is a vortex that appears when you die. It comes for your life energies, and takes them up." Mandee flicked her tail, sending a cascade of flickering stars across the rug. "After a short time of total black, where I saw, felt, heard, and scented nothing, I felt myself rise. My senses returned, but all was hazy and cloudy. My memories began to fade as The Rift lifted me from my body, then I saw Momma crying."

"You saw her after the Big Sleep took you?" Khan asked in total stupefied amazement. "How?"

"I think all of us can see briefly when our energies leave our bodies. But some may see little and some may see more. When I saw Momma, I became scared. I was leaving her, and I couldn't bear it. I fought The Vortex. It yanked at me like mamas do with kittens, but I fought. The room cleared, and it closed and left. I clung to my body."

"But you went in the fire!" Khan exclaimed, aghast.

"Yes, and I watched my body turn to ash," Mandee flattened her ears. "It looked horrific, but I felt nothing. I stayed with the ashes, even when they went into that tin. There I stayed."

"How did you know you'd see Momma again?" Munchkin asked in his gravelly voice. "You didn't tell us how."

"I heard the talk. Momma told me I'd be coming home, no matter what, so I had to stay with my body."

"Where did The Rift go?" Warlocke asked, batting at any stars that floated past him.

"I don't know," Mandee lashed her tail. Stars flared and crackled, shooting into the dark room. "But I don't want to be recycled and reborn. I want to stay here."

"Reborn? Like into a newborn kitten?" Khan asked, fascinated, yet, at the same moment, scared of the starry halo surrounding Mandee.

"Yes." Mandee nodded. "I am glad to be home."

"I can't wait to tell Black," Khan said with excitement. "Can you go see him?"

"I don't know. I think I may be confined to this room or the house, but I may try." Mandee turned her attention to Indy. "But for now, I have something I must do."

"What?"

"Payback time," she growled, and darted across the room, heading for Indy. Her halo scintillated with expended energy. Indy wailed in alarm, then fled the room. Mandee slapped his rump, and sparks exploded. Indy yowled and raced around, trying to hide. But Mandee followed him to his every hiding place. Khan broke up with feline laughter. Phantom joined him. Munchkin sat up in his bed, thoroughly amused.

"So he gets what he deserves after harassing her when she was so sick? This will be amusing."

"Fun, fun!" Warlocke danced in Mandee's wake, batting at stars that faded and winked out like bubbles in a breeze.

All that night and the next day, Mandee gleefully chased Indy around the house. He dashed from her, body low to the ground, eyes wide, as he desperately tried to find a safe refuge from her attacks. He uttered no sounds. Momma sat at the computer, eyeing Indy as he scurried back and forth in a witless rush.

"Indy, what is wrong with you?" she asked. "Have a bug up your butt today?"

He ignored her completely. Momma lifted a brow, and shook her head with confusion. Khan sat, watching from the other computer chair. Warlocke lay on one of the dining room chairs, while Phantom sat under the table. Indy shot into the kitchen, tail tucked, then whirled and fled back out. Mandee's transparent form followed.

"Momma can't see Mandee." Khan glanced at his buddy. "Why?"

"I don't know," Phantom replied. "It makes no sense. She struggled to be with Momma, but Momma has no idea."

"How long will she keep chasing him?" Warlocke asked, twitching his silver-touched black tail.

"Maybe forever," Phantom answered with a snort. "Serves him right for how he acts."

To Khan's surprise, the chase lasted only half of a mooncycle. Indy finally figured out that the shocks Mandee dealt with her paws hurt very little. They exploded with light and sound, but not much else. He halted one day in the hall, turned, and faced her.

"I'm not running anymore," he puffed angrily through his nose. Mandee sat down.

"You're no fun," she hissed, then returned to the livingroom. "I need to replenish my energies."

From that day on, she stayed in her tin most of the time. She never tried to leave the house to visit Black, no matter how often Khan asked. One night, many mooncycles later, he demanded to talk to her. She emerged, her halo dim, stars few, but her eyes sparkled bright.

"Why can't you try to see Black? I haven't seen him in a while. Momma has been too busy to take me outside, and when she does, he's not around."

"I'm tired," she complained. "Why doesn't Phantom tell him about me?"

"Phantom won't talk to him unless I'm there."

"I'm sorry, but I am too tired to try."

"Tired? How can you be tired?"

"I don't know," Mandee lamented. "But I am. I save my energy so I can come out and sit with Momma at night."

"But she can't sense you at all."

"I went to her room one night. I walked on her bed and on her feet like I used to. She felt it, and knows I am here."

"She doesn't act like it," Khan argued. "She still cries sometimes."

"Yes, but she talks to me. She holds my tin and talks to me. I know." Mandee wavered. "I must go. Good night."

She faded, and vanished into her tin. Khan sat, lashing his tail, confused. Sighing, he leaped on the sofa, and curled up to nap.

"NO!"

The cry jolted Khan from his nap, and brought Phantom and Warlocke in the livingroom on the run. Munchkin sat up abruptly in his catbed.

"Can't a cat get any sleep?" he growled.

"No!" The wail echoed in the house again. Khan faced the cabinet housing Mandee's tin. It glowed bright, and, to his horror, just outside the glass, floated a long shining blue streak. It pulsed in all shades of blue, and formed an oblong shape that split lengthwise. The opening gleamed bright. Khan glimpsed inside, but saw only swirling bright lights in whites and blues of every shade. Suddenly, Mandee rose out of her tin.

"No, please!" she wailed. She kicked and twisted, but some unseen force gripped the scruff of her neck. Stars flared and shot from her body, quickly dying in the black room. Mandee glanced at Khan.

"Help me! Don't let it take me!"

"What can I do?" Khan protested, his forefeet shifting with agitation.

"I don't knooooow! Moooommmmaaaa!" Mandee howled, as the force swept her up and into the opening. Khan caught another brief look into The Rift. White ghostly shapes floated among puffy blue swirls and clouds. Mandee's colors faded, and she turned translucent white. The Rift closed, and vanished with an audible pop.

Khan stared in shock, breathing heavily.

"Great smoking doots!" Phantom exclaimed, his eyes dilated to maximum. "What happened?"

"She's gone," Khan said with a yowl. "It took her away!"

"I'm glad of it," Indy grumbled from behind the chair.

"Shut up," Phantom snarled.

"She should never have been here," Indy retorted.

"How do you know, you witless idiot?" Phantom snapped, rising to his feet. "You never go anywhere, or talk to anyone!"

"Leave him be." Khan hurried to his friend, wishing to avert a real fight. "He has a point. Even she said she shouldn't be here, remember?"

"Yes," Phantom agreed, lashed his tail, and sat back down.

"Let's sleep, and forget it."

"Yeah, sure." Phantom jumped to the floor. "I'm getting a snack."

Khan watched his buddy leave before curling up on the sofa. He tried to rationalize all that happened since that day Momma brought home Mandee's tin. He desperately wanted to speak to Black.

The next evening, Phantom sauntered into the house, bearing a nasty scratch on his nose and ear. Khan sniffed the scratches, and Phantom shook his head.

"It's no big deal."

"Right," Khan sniffed him all over. "You have scratches all over you. You were fighting again! With who? I can't scent your opponent."

"Does it matter? I washed up after the fight. It was no big deal." Phantom abruptly walked away, lashing his tail. Khan left him alone, sensing his friend's deep agitation. He knew Mandee's vanishing into The Vortex upset Phantom more than the big cat let on. Khan longed to speak to Black about all this, but the black cat did not respond to his calls when he went out on his harness a few days later, and Phantom remained mysteriously evasive whenever Khan asked him if he saw Black outside anymore. Khan worried that someone took Black away.

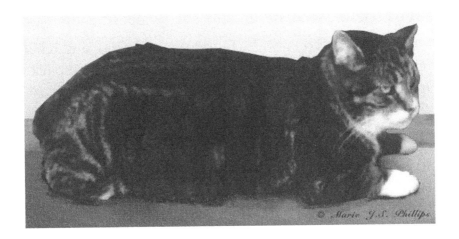

© Marie J.S. Phillips

## CHAPTER 13: MUNCHKIN'S BATTLE

Mooncycles passed, and Full Leaf turned to Leaf Fall. Black remained mysteriously absent. Khan worried about his old friend, but adjusted to the inevitable. Leaf Fall turned to No Leaf season. One bitter cold day, a ruckus erupted outside on the back porch. Khan listened, alert, recognizing Munchkin's wail of anger, amid a stranger's answering snarls. Momma raced out into the cold, and brought Munchkin into the house. Phantom darted in after them. Uncharacteristically angry, Munchkin wriggled in her grasp as Momma carried him.

"Why are you fighting, Munchie?" Momma asked. Khan followed, repeating the question.

"You never fight," Khan remarked. "Why do you attack that other cat?"

"I hate that stranger!" he snarled. Momma put him down on the bathroom floor. Phantom joined him, as Momma fussed over both. Khan saw Munchkin's deep puncture wounds, and his eyes widened.

"He got you good," Phantom remarked, and Khan sniffed Munchkin's wounded shoulder. He pulled back in alarm.

"It smells wrong!"

"What about mine?" Phantom asked, turning his rump to his buddy. Khan moved to sniff Phantom's small rump wound.

"It doesn't smell bad," Khan said, and sat down. Momma vigorously washed Munchkin's shoulder, pouring funny stuff that foamed into the punctures.

"I hate him," Munchkin growled. "He should go away."

"I agree, but he's so sick that he'll likely die soon anyway. You should just leave him alone."

"He's mean, and thinks he owns this place," Munchkin protested. "He doesn't! It's our home."

"I know, but one fight was enough for me when I scented the wrongness of him," Phantom argued. "I can kick his butt, but he doesn't care, and keeps coming back."

"I hate him."

"So do I, but he smells so wrong. We could catch that wrongness from him," Phantom warned. "You should leave him alone."

"How do you know we can catch the wrongness? A disease?"

"Yes," Phantom confirmed. "He is dangerous. I just feel it."

"I hate him," Munchkin growled, struggling against Momma's first-aid care. "He must not be allowed to stay here."

No matter how much Phantom and Khan tried to talk Munchkin out of it, Munchkin continued to attack the stray tomcat. One day, the stranger did not return, and Munchkin relaxed his vigil as the days warmed into Leaf Bloom. The tension left the household, and Khan felt happy the stranger finally vanished from the area. Full Leaf season brought quiet to Khan's life, but he worried about Black. Normally, he saw Black often during the hot time of year, but he knew he might never see Black again. Leaf Fall season arrived. One morning, Khan sauntered downstairs to find Munchkin lying beside the water dish, weak and sick.

"Are you all right?"

"No," Munchkin raised his head. "I feel weak, and can't get enough water. I hurt inside."

"Oh, no," Khan mewled, as Munchkin suddenly lurched to his feet.

"I have to do pee."

"No! The litter box is over there!" Khan cried after him. Munchkin walked into the bathroom, then urinated on the towel spread out on the floor by the tub. Poppy saw Munchkin's naughty act, and bellowed for Momma, who came in on the run, groggy and disoriented from sleep.

"Why did you do that?" Khan asked, when Munchkin returned to the water dish. He collapsed, yet tried to drink more water. Khan sniffed noses with him, and scented something wrong, something bad. His heart fluttered, and sank to his tail.

"To show Momma I feel bad," Munchkin murmured.

Later that day, much to Khan's dismay, Momma took Munchkin to the cat doctor. She returned home in a panic, and grabbed Phantom, stuffed him in a carrier, and hurried from the house. Khan paced, mewling in fear. What happened? Momma returned shortly, with Phantom, hugging him as she let him out of the carrier.

"What is going on?" Khan asked his friend.

"Momma had me tested for something called Feline AIDS!" Phantom answered, his tail still bushy with fear. "Munchkin got it from that sick stranger. I could have gotten it, too, from the bites! I am lucky. Munchkin also has something else, called can-cer. It's very bad."

Khan sat, shocked. All that day, Momma paced, crying. Khan knew the Big Sleep waited to claim another of his family. Munchkin never returned home, and, days later, another little tin joined Mandee's in the livingroom. Momma cried again, and Khan rubbed against her. Phantom hurried to his side.

"I am here," he purred. "Me and Phantom."

"Me, too," Warlocke said, joining them. Together, they circled Momma and purred, making her smile and hug each of them. Khan stared at the tin, and all the memories of that night over a suncycle ago returned in a rush. He suddenly realized that in his few Leaf Fall outings, he missed Black and needed to know what happened to him. When Momma left the room, Khan whirled on Phantom.

"Do you ever see Black anymore? Is he sick? Did someone take him away?"

"Yes, lots of times, " Phantom admitted. "He is still around."

"And you never told me?" Khan's heart sang with joy, but anger battled that happiness."Even though you knew I missed him?"

"I am sorry. I thought it better this way, I don't speak to him. He avoids me."

"Why? Are you fighting with him again? Is that why he never came to see me when I'm outside?" Khan raised a paw, hissing his anger."You let me think someone took him away?"

"Hey, no! You never asked." Phantom pulled back. "I see him once in a while, but I don't fight."

"You're lying," Khan growled. "Why else would he not come?"

"I'm sorry," Phantom hung his head in shame. "I did chase him a few times. I didn't mean it, but I think he took it too serious, and right after Mandee went into The Vortex, we had a big argument."

"The night you came home with all those scratches!" Khan glared at his buddy.

"I am sorry," Phantom mewled.

"Now he won't come to see me," Khan cuffed his friend hard. "You must go apologize. I want to talk to him next time I go outside."

"All right. For you, I will," Phantom agreed, and jumped on the sofa to nap."Forgive me?"

"Yes, but only if you get Black to see me."

"I promise." Phantom yawned. Khan joined him, but sleep eluded him. He uncurled, tucked his feet underneath him, and watched Munchkin's tin. He expected it to glow any moment, but nothing happened. He lay his head down after a night's long vigil and sighed in a long twitter. Beside him, Phantom rolled over.

"What is wrong?"

"I thought Munchkin would come back like Mandee did."

"He didn't."

"I know, but why? I don't understand why he didn't."

"I'm glad he didn't," Indy grumbled from behind the chair.

"Good thing for you. You harassed him worse than you did Mandee," Khan growled. "He may have hit you with more than just sparks."

"Well, he didn't. I'm glad of it."

"I wish he would come back," Warlocke said, from his spot on the chair. "I miss him."

Khan agreed with a silent nod, and fell asleep with his eyes on Munchkin's box. Night after night for a full mooncycle, he watched and waited, but the red, white-flowered tin remained dark. He wished so much to speak to Black about all this, and tried convincing Momma to take him out on his harness. She did not understand, even when he rushed to her side when she opened the drawer where she kept his harness stored. He pawed the straps, and uttered his soft meow. Momma tousled his ears.

"Not today, sweetie. I'm too busy, and it's still cold out there," she said, day after day.

Finally, Momma took him out on a warm day during early Leaf Bloom. Breezes blew across the grass, while Momma hooked his long lead to a spike in the ground. She and Poppy relaxed on white loungers. Khan drank in the glorious day, scanning the yard and scenting the wind. To his delight, the familiar black shape materialized at the edge of the lawn. Khan strained at the end of his lead.

"Black! Black! Please! Come see me!"

Black halted, looked up, then turned up the lawn. Phantom appeared from the opposite side, and trotted over. Black slowed down, eyeing Khan's huge buddy, but walked up to Khan.

"Black! Are you all right? Where have you been?" Khan asked, his tail raised up behind him in the characteristic hook.

"I am fine," Black answered, touching noses with Khan. Phantom trotted up, and Black backed up a step.

"Black, stay," Phantom said, and sat down. "I told you I was sorry. I meant it."

"I can't help being a bit cautious, even after we spoke a mooncycle ago. You hurt me bad enough that I had to go to the cat doctor. I wasn't let out let out for a long time. The new cat in the house, Oscar, hates me, and we fought a lot, which slowed my recovery. When I healed enough, I left quickly, but it took a while."

"You hurt him that badly?" Khan hissed, and turned to Phantom.

"I didn't mean it, really," Phantom dropped his head, ears down with shame. "I got carried away, especially with what went on then with Mandee. I guess I took it out on him"

"No excuse," Khan growled. "You never said you hurt him bad enough to go to the cat doctor. I don't care what was going on then. That was no excuse to rip into my friend."

Black sat down.

"What went on when?" he asked, curiosity burning in his eyes. Khan gazed at him, and saw a knowing spark in his old friend's eyes.

"You know!" Khan glanced at Phantom. "Did you tell him?"

"No." Phantom flattened his ears, shame in every line of his strong body.

"Munchkin did, but that was right before I was hurt. It was the cause of the argument between Phantom and me. I was angry Phantom never told me about her spiritual return made the mistake of attacking him in my outrage, so what happened was partly my fault."
Black's face furrowed into a worried frown. "Where is

Munchkin? I was worried about him, but have not seen him for mooncycles."

"He went to the Big Sleep," Khan answered, then rushed ahead. "He's in a tin, like Mandee, but he never came back! Why? Why didn't he come back but Mandee did?"

"There is no easy answer, Kid," Black answered softly, his expression thoughtful. "Though I've earned a lot recently about such things, I find it hard to believe what you say really happened."

"It did," Phantom growled. "You don't believe us? Then why did you get so mad at me just because I didn't tell you about it? We all saw her. Ask Indy sometime, if he'll talk to you through the windows. He felt her wrath."

"She said it's true that we don't see, scent, hear, or feel after the Big Sleep takes us, but it doesn't stay that way. She said you sort of wake in a daze, and then The Rift takes you," Khan added. "She said she was able to come back because she saw our momma crying, and somehow she was able to resist."

"I wish I had spoken to her," Black sighed. Phantom's angry glare vanished, and he looked away.

"I tried to get her to find you, but after she chased Indy around for days, she became very tired, and only came out to sit with Momma at night." Khan explained. "Then, one night, The Rift returned, lifted her up like a naughty kitten, and took her away."

"She violated natural laws," Black said. "I talked to an old tomcat down the street about this. He said that life energy recycles, and is reborn into new life. What Mandee did was defy the natural way. He said The Rift, or Vortex, as he called it, always wins in the end."

"What about me?" Phantom commented. "We all think Demon passed into me. Why didn't any Rift come to take him away? I would have remembered that."

"That is different," Black said. "He was reborn, in a way, by mingling his life energy with yours. You've had accidents, yet rebounded with much energy and life. You escaped the danger from that sick stray. Ever wonder about that?"

"No," Phantom flicked his tail, and fell silent.

"While I was still nursing from my mama, she said we are reborn. After my littlest brother died, she explained it to us," a new voice joined the conversation. Khan turned to see Black's old housemate, grey-and-white Rumple, saunter over to the group. Khan met him with a nose sniff and raised tail.

"Hello! You should visit more often."

"I would, but your friend there hates me."

"No," Khan growled at Phantom, who stood up, fur rising, in an aggressive posture. "Let him stay."

Phantom sat back down, grumbling. Khan glared at him, then returned his attention to the newcomer.

"You know of these things?"

"Some, but I haven't experienced them myself. But after my brother died, my mama explained how The Vortex works. It takes our life essence when we die, and cycles it into a new kitten. She said that he might come back through her as a new kitten, but might also be born of a completely different mama."

"Sorry about your brother," Khan murmured.

"It's O.K. He was always weak, and got sick. Mama said it happens."

"Not fair to die as a kitten," Khan muttered, chattering his teeth.

"No, I guess it is not, but it's worse when you're older and have a loving human momma. But sometimes, when our human mommas love us so much, and we love them, we can escape The Vortex for a while. It always comes for us eventually, but she also said that sometimes, that love bond influences The Vortex, and when we are reborn, our mommas find us again as new kittens." Rumple responded.

"Really?" Khan gasped. "Will Mandee come back to us as a new kitten?"

"Maybe, maybe not. So much has to go right, and nobody really understands how it all works. My little brother never came back, and even if he did, we'd not know it at all." Rumple yawned. "I'm going to go hunting. It's been interesting." He glanced at Black. "I am sorry Oscar hates you so much. Momma has taken his side in all this. I am sorry." With that, he trotted across the lawn and down into the woods.

"Its alright, Rumple. I'll be fine." Black called after his friend. Khan stared after Rumple, then looked at Phantom.

"Don't you speak to other cats around here? Why don't you know that stuff? Especially about Black's situation?"

"I stay in my yard, and protect it," Phantom retorted. "I never thought to do that, but I am sorry about all of it."

"No matter," Khan said, and Phantom relaxed. "It's all done and over with."

"He explained it well. As much as you all loved Munchkin, the pull wasn't strong enough. The bond was strong enough to let Mandee return as an apparition, but, obviously, it was not strong enough to allow her to come back here reborn." Black rose, and stretched. "I'm hungry. Time to visit the neighbors and beg for some good snacks!"

"You're always hungry," Khan teased, feeling worry for his old friend, but he also knew Black took good care of himself all his life.

"Good day, my friend. I hope you found the answers you sought." Black turned, and trotted away.

"I think so," Khan whispered, then hurried over to Momma's chair. Phantom followed him. Khan jumped up, and cuddled at her feet, and Phantom joined him. Fears raced through him. Khan met his pal's sea-green gaze, and saw sorrow, shame, and fear gleaming in Phantom's wide eyes. Momma stroked both of them, and Khan took solace in her touch.

"I hope many, many suncycles pass before the Big Sleep forces me away from Momma and you," Khan mewed, head-butting Phantom's shoulder.

"I feel the same way," Phantom purred raggedly. Khan leaned into Momma, kneading her leg. He never ever wanted to leave Momma, but knew when the Big Sleep came for him, no choices lay ahead for him.

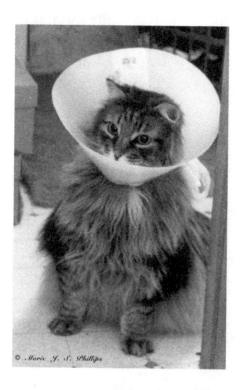

© Marie J. S. Phillips

# CHAPTER 14: SUDDEN ILLNESS

Slowly, life returned again to normal, but Khan never let the memories fade into nothing. He often wondered about Mandee's return as a spirit, and Munchkin's lack of such activity. Khan hated to see Momma so sad, and wished to help her be happy again. He ate, and put on weight, and during the cold snow season, he proudly flaunted his seventeen pounds of robust body, reveling in his luxurious coat, which grew in thick and soft. Momma groomed him with pride. Her delight in his good health radiated strongly to him.

"You look great! Your britches are full and golden. I have never seen your coat so beautiful before," Phantom said one day, as the wind howled outside, driving before it heavy snow. "The picture of the perfect Maine Coon. Momma is very proud."

"I feel great, too," Khan said, and started a game of wrestling.

The snow season turned to Leaf Bloom. On a warm morning, Phantom pulled up in a wrestling bout, sat down, and gazed at him.

"What?" Khan twitched his tail, legs in the air.

"You're losing weight again."

"So? What else is new?"

"Momma isn't going to like it if it continues."

"But I eat well!" Khan protested.

To his dismay, Khan endured more cat doctor visits as his weight slowly dropped again, despite his good eating habits. One sunny morning, Momma found a strange lump on Khan's leg.

"What is this?" she asked, trying to pull it off. "A matt?"

"Hey, that hurts!" Khan nipped her. A flurry of cat doctor visits followed, and Khan endured them, but his own fear grew. Momma seemed very concerned. In early Full Leaf, Momma brought him at the cat doctor for perhaps the tenth time.

"Bye, sweetie. Be a good boy," Momma said, and left him with the cat nurses. He waited in a cage, nervous but not frightened. Gently, one of the nurses pulled Khan from his cage, and prepared him for the removal of the funny growth on his back leg. They spoke in soothing voices, and, as he drifted off to slumber, he felt someone touching the lump on his leg. Khan tried twitching his leg, but fell asleep instead. When he woke up, they tied a big collar around his head, and placed him in his cage.

"Nooo!" he wailed. "Take it off. I can't see anything."

"Sorry, Big Guy," the cat nurse said. "You must wear this so you won't bother your stitches."

Khan mewled as she put him in the familiar carrier. The collar bumped the sides, jolting his neck. Momma picked him up from that surgery, and he growled at the collar the entire ride home. He hated how it felt.

"Oh, baby, what's the matter? You mad at Momma?"

"No, Momma. Take it off?" Khan asked, knowing she did not understand. He settled down with a growling mutter. Once home, he left the carrier, glad to be home, but tried removing the collar by rubbing it on doorframes. He growled, and Momma laughed.

"So it's that thing you hate? I am sorry, sweetie. You must wear it."

Khan tried to ignore the collar, especially when the other cats snickered. Momma chuckled, petting him.

"My little Hooverhead!"

"Hooverhead!" Phantom laughed. "Like the vacuum cleaners on TV?"

Khan ignored him. The next day, as Momma and Poppy ate dinner, Khan struggled to shove the collar off, but it soon tightened further around his neck. With a growl, he sat on the dining room floor, reached up with a back paw, hooked his claws into the collar, then twisted and pulled with all his strength. Momma stared at him in shock, but before she moved to stop him, Khan popped the hated collar off in one swift motion. He shook his head, and looked at Momma, thoroughly pleased with himself, as the collar rolled down the hallway.

"Don't put it back, please!"

"If you hate it that much, you can keep it off." Momma laughed, and returned to eating. Proud of his accomplishment, Khan hurried to his dish. He wobbled a bit, still weakened by the surgery, but he felt determined to reclaim his health.

Khan ate, and regained strength, and soon felt himself again; however, he failed to keep weight on. As the days warmed, Khan felt uncomfortable lying down sometimes. His joints rubbed the floor.

"You're getting thin," Phantom remarked one day. "You are eating, right? Maybe you have what I have."

"Yes, I am eating, but I always have the runny poops. Momma cut off my beautiful britches," Khan lamented, glancing back at his shaved rear end. "And I have to take those pills. What do you have?"

"Momma calls it hy-hyper–thy-thyroidism. If you just swallow the pills, you'd never taste them. The babyfood is wonderful. I take mine just fine."

"You're a pig cat, as Momma says so often."

"And I am healthy, too," Phantom reminded him. "Even if I am getting older. We are ten suncycles old now."

"Yes, but not so old," Khan said. "But I am eating. Why am I getting thin again?

"I don't know." Phantom sniffed him all over. "You don't smell bad."

Khan twitched his tail, and decided not to worry. He dropped weight many times before, and always put it back. Middle Full Leaf brought warm wonderful days, and Momma let him go outdoors on his harness. During family picnics, he claimed a chair for himself, and watched everything with delight. Sometimes he and Phantom wrestled until the harness lead tangled up too much. At one such picnic, a big black dog trotted into the yard, approaching Poppy, panting, and begging for attention.

"How dare he!" Phantom suddenly growled. "Poppy is ours!"

Phantom puffed up, head down in stalk mode, and advanced on the dog. Khan watched, amused, as the dog trotted away, giving Phantom a wide berth. Phantom followed at a run, and Khan jumped from the chair, unable to resist the chase. The dog spun around, surprise in his eyes, and he gazed at Phantom and Khan. For many moments, Khan and Phantom stood rock-still, until the dog laid down. Khan and Phantom did likewise, and enjoyed a wonderful staring contest. After a long interval, the dog finally rose to his feet and slowly walked out of the yard, stopping every few paces to glance back to Khan and Phantom.

"Run, dog, run!" Phantom urged, his muscles twitching, ready for a good chase, but the dog ambled away. Khan blinked at his buddy.

"That was fun!"

"Not as fun as it could have been. If he ran, I'd have chased him, and clawed his butt!" Phantom purred. "The audacity of trying to make nice with our poppy! But he seemed like a gentle sort. Those aren't as fun to scratch."

"No?"

"The best ones are the pompous fools who think all cats are prey," Phantom replied, a growl in his tones. "I love backing into the bushes, and luring them into range. Remember when those two came at me that time? Momma came out and praised me! I told you I could do this. Dogs give our yard a wide berth now."

"Why did the black one come?"

"Never saw him before," Phantom sneezed in mirth. "He may not come back, but if he does, I won't be so nice next time."

Khan joined him in feline laughter, and they basked together in the afternoon sun.

Two moon cycles after that fun-filled day, Khan woke feeling ill. He blinked his eyes, trying to clear away a sticky film. He rebuffed Phantom's overtures to play.

"What is wrong?" Phantom asked, surprise in his eyes.

Khan sneezed, then yawned.

"Feel sick."

"You have a cat cold." Phantom lay beside Khan. Days went by, and Khan's worried Momma put him in the carrier, and took him to the cat doctor again. Khan bleated protests, fearing the Big Sleep.

"They don't make cats go to the Big Sleep for a cold," Phantom said, as Momma carried his carrier out of the house. Khan knew his best friend was right, and relaxed. Momma brought him home after the cat doctor examined him. He felt better the next day, and began eating again, allowing Momma to give him medications.

One morning, the medication gave him a bad bellyache. He ran from the kitchen to lie on his favorite chair. Suddenly, his belly twisted, and the food and medicine came up. Khan jumped to the floor, and sat in a hunched position, wanting the ache to pass soon. He shifted positions, then stood, and went upstairs to rest on the hallway rug. Momma came up, patted his head, and went into the library. Khan suddenly needed to use the litterbox, and ran to the one in the library. He barely made it. Cramps wracked his system, and he left the box to huddle at the top of the stairs. Momma halted on her way down, a worried look on her face.

"Are you OK, my big bear?"

"No," Khan mewed his answer.

Khan lost his appetite, and no matter what Momma did that afternoon, he threw up. It burned, and he hated the messy results. He never before experienced such sickness of the stomach. Phantom's eyes widened in alarm as he came in from outside. He greeted Khan with a nose sniff.

"You are really sick. I can scent it now. I am scared for you. I've never seen you throw up so much," Phantom commented, and gently nuzzled him. Warlocke rubbed against him, concern in his soft purr. Even Indy peered at him with wide eyes. Khan quailed inwardly, recalling the day he scented the wrongness in Munchkin.

"Is it the same?" he asked Phantom in a pitiful mewl. "Do I smell like Munchkin?"

"Not exactly the same." Phantom licked Khan's head. "But I don't know why."

Khan huddled in his chair, sick and scared, and unable to keep anything in his stomach.

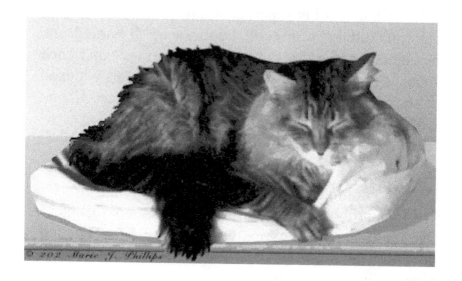

# CHAPTER 15: THE OPERATION

The next morning, Momma took him to the cat doctor, where he received shots. He felt better for one day, then the stomach cramps and nausea returned in a rush. Momma brought him back to the doctor the next morning. Khan huddled miserably in his carrier, resisting when Momma and the doctor tried to pull him out. He lost strength quickly, and they gently took him out. The doctor examined him thoroughly, gently running his hands expertly over Khan's gaunt frame.

"We have to keep him," the cat doctor said, picking him up off the exam table. "He is very dehydrated. Call us in the morning to check on him."

"I will," Momma said, a quaver in her voice. She kissed Khan's head, then the doctor carried him out of the room. He bleated, as terror coursed through him. The doctor placed him in a cage, sticking tubes and needles into him. His joints hurt, no matter how he lay, and he realized how much weight he lost. His mind spun with confusion and pain.

"We'll take care of you, Big Guy," the doctor said, and patted his head. "My wife is a wonderful surgeon."

Khan bleated. Surgeon? What was that?

The day passed slowly, but soon nightfall arrived. The bustling Animal Hospital quieted down, and only the barking and meowing of his fellow caged patients echoed in the building. He saw only one human, who checked in on them every so often.

"Why did Momma leave me here again?" he mewed in the dark of the night. He refused to eat. He wanted to sleep, rest, and close this place from his mind forever. The days melded into each other, and he remembered his early days at the shelter.

"Why did you leave me here, Momma? Why?" he mewled, ignoring all the other patients. "What will happen to me now?"

"You will be all right. The doctors will take good care of you." A voice soothed him out of the dark. A grey-brown tabby cat materialized out of the gloom, and perched on the exam table near Khan's cage. Khan lifted his head, his mind clearing at the hauntingly familiar feline voice.

"Who is there?" Khan faced the tabby.

"Greetings. I am Oliver. Oh! Hello, Khan. It's good to talk to you after all these years. It is a shame that it must be under such circumstances."

"Hello, Oliver." Khan answered, recognizing the resident hospital cat. "Glad to see you, too. You shouldn't be back here."

"I know, but I live here, remember? The doc doesn't get that upset with me because I donate my blood to help other cats, but I don't want to cause big trouble with the patients. I know you're scared. You've never stayed here beyond overnight before. But it will be all right." Oliver jumped down to the floor, heading for the door. "I also shouldn't be back here too long. The other cats get upset, but you sounded so forlorn, I came back to talk to you."

"I miss my momma." Khan mewled, feeling like a scared kitten. "I feel so bad, too. I think the Big Sleep will take me, and I'll never see her again."

"I know. I am sure your momma misses you, too. Don't worry. The doctors here will make you feel better. The Big Sleep is not coming for you yet." Oliver slipped through the doorway. Khan lay his head down, exhausted by the exchange, hoping Oliver spoke the truth, not only words of comfort. He wanted his momma.

One bright morning, they took him from his cage, and placed him on a blanket. He trembled with fear until a familiar voice and scent filtered past his senses. Momma! He purred, relaxed. Finally, something felt right with the world. She embraced him gently. Her

KHAN: A MAINE COON

voice quavered with sobs, bringing his mind out of its spiraling pain and confusion.

"Why cry, Momma?" he purred.

"Oh, Khan, my baby, please be strong. They're gonna fix you up, honey bear. You'll come home soon, no matter what happens. No matter what, you'll be home soon." Momma sobbed a bit, then continued. "Don't leave me, sweet one -- please don't leave me!"

Khan purred raggedly, confused by her words, wanting to sleep, cuddled in her arms, until the pain went away. He wished to sleep, sleep for . . . his mind hiccuped, and he stopped his thoughts. Forever! Like the Big Sleep! She cried because she feared he might never scent, see, or hear her again, ever. She feared his coming home in a little tin, like Mandee and Munchkin! His heart leaped. He wanted to stay with her, and not be reborn in a new kitten, to end up with some strange human momma. He purred louder, even when the technician returned to the room. He realized his momma loved him, never abandoned him, and wanted him back home. She wanted him to be strong, to fight. As the technician took Khan away from his momma, he resolved to battle the sickness that kept him here.

Later that day, the cat surgeon came for him. She handled him gently, speaking to him in soothing tones. He fought fears as the cat surgeon and her technicians injected him with medicines that forced him to sleep. When he awoke, pain wracked his body, but he remembered his momma's last words.

"Don't leave me!" floated in his mind. He fought the nausea and vomiting that dehydrated his body and shaved more pounds off his gaunt frame. The stitches down his naked belly pulled at his skin, and he huddled in his bedding, trying to keep it warm. The doctor and his nurses injected him with medicines, every day, and, slowly, the nausea diminished. The awful painful retching stopped, and his surgical incision hurt less.

On the third morning, the resident hospital cat sauntered into the back room. Khan recognized Oliver, but felt too weak to even call out to the tabby. He wondered why Oliver wandered back here. He knew the grey-brown tabby preferred the reception area, where he received attention from all the humans out there. Oliver paused, and looked up at Khan.

"You are looking better. Hungry yet?"

"Well, I don't think so," Khan responded, then paused. His stomach grumbled, and he felt hungry for the first time in many days.

"Maybe I am," Khan said. "How did you know?"

"I heard your stomach growling when I came in. Eat, and recover well." Oliver twitched his whiskers.

"I will," Khan answered softly.

"I told you The Big Sleep was not coming for you," Oliver meowed, and left the room.

On the fourth morning, Khan ate what the technicians offered him. The food tasted good, and settled in his stomach. They showered him with praise, and seemed as delighted as he when the food stayed down. To his surprise, on the third day he ate, they took him from his cage, and placed him in the familiar carrier. His heart spun with joy.

"Momma!" he mewed. He scented the familiar vehicle, heard his momma's voice as she babbled to him. Once inside the home he loved so well, Khan toddled out of the carrier. Phantom rushed up to him, eagerly sniffing his nose.

"Where have you been?"

"At the doctor's," Khan answered. "They made me feel better, but I am so glad I am home."

"Me, too. I missed you. I thought, I thought . . ." Phantom trailed off.

"I know. I thought it was the Big Sleep for me, too," Khan said, and rubbed his buddy's face with his. "But Oliver said it was not time for me to go to the Big Sleep."

"Glad he was right." Phantom flicked an ear. "What did they do that took so long?"

"They went inside me. Look at my poor belly."

Khan rolled over and exposed his bare belly. The incision ran from chest to lower abdomen, shining a bright pink. Phantom stared in astonishment, then sniffed the entire length of Khan's belly.

"What did they do to you?" Phantom asked in a soft sad mew.

"I'm not sure. I heard the doctor call it exploratory something. And said the word bi-op-sy many times." Khan slowly sat up. "I do feel better now. So whatever they did, helped me."

"I am so glad you're home," Phantom said, then turned, and trotted to the kitchen to the food bowls, tail high. Khan followed, but staggered. Momma picked him up gently, hugged him, and put him in a large cage, with a soft bed, food, and a small litter box. Khan sagged to the bed in exhaustion, and nibbled the food offering before going to sleep.

## CHAPTER 16: OUTDOORS AT CHRISTMAS

As the days passed, Khan slowly gained strength. Before long, he felt strong enough to play with his best friend. Phantom sometimes forgot his strength, and Khan hissed warnings.

"Careful! That hurt!"

"Sorry!" Phantom sat down apologetically each time. A moon cycle passed, and Momma brought down from the enticing-yet-off-limits attic his favorite things -- the Christmas Tree and all the wonderful decorations. Momma joyfully hung bright lights and garlands high out of Khan's reach. Excitement coursed through his gaunt weak body as the tree stood, decorated, lights shining, waiting for him to start his favorite game of ripping the ornaments off the Christmas Tree. He batted the bright balls and baubles, shaking the tree. Warlocke purred in delight, joining in the fun. Momma's quick steps stopped the game, and Khan waited for the rebuke, but Momma only laughed softly and hugged him.

"Play, honey bear. Enjoy every moment," she said, and walked back to her chair at the computer. Surprised, Khan glanced at Warlocke, then resumed the game. Again, Momma appeared, and Khan expected a scolding, but one never erupted from Momma. She smiled, and hugged him again.

"Why isn't she yelling at us?" Warlocke asked, batting at a clear plastic ball. The shiny stuff inside wiggled, enticing him to smack harder.

"I don't know,' Khan said, eyeing a red lumpy ball, "but I am not taking any chances. If she comes back, we stop."

Khan enjoyed the games, and the wonderful changes these decorations brought to his home. His belly betrayed him once in a while, scaring Momma, upsetting Phantom, but Khan rested on those days, then rebounded, tolerating all the nasty medicines Momma gave to him. He endured the regular visits to the cat doctor for his check-ups and shots. He always felt better after his shots, eating well, and pleasing Momma.

One warm day, his momma opened the drawer of the hutch. Khan heard the familiar jangle of his harness, and darted to his momma's side.

"Go outside?" he mewed. "Oh, please! We go outside?"

"Yes, my honey bear, we are going outside."
Momma put the harness on him, and led him out into
the unusually warm No Leaf day. Brave annuals, left
over from Full Leaf, bloomed in defiance of the season.
The breeze blew in from the south, full of tantalizing
scents. Joy flooded Khan's body, and he led Momma
around, investigating his beloved yard. Phantom
followed.

"I missed this so much," Khan meowed. "I am so
happy."

Suddenly, Khan spied a familiar figure across the
lawn. His tail rose above his back, and he trotted toward
the black cat, dragging his momma along. Phantom
surged ahead, and Khan sensed some jealousy. Black
stood defensively as Phantom faced him, tall and
threatening.

"Phantom, no!" Khan pushed past his buddy,
stalling any attack by Phantom. "Didn't you learn
anything? Please, don't fight."

"I wasn't going to hurt him," Phantom thrust his
whiskers forward. "We have an understanding."

"Black!" Khan reached his friend, and touched
noses with him.

"Khan?" Black sniffed Khan's nose in disbelief.
"Phantom told me you were very ill."

"I was, but I feel better now. I have something
called can-cer."

"That is a bad disease." Black Satin tilted his ears
back, before flicking them forward along with his

whiskers. "You look well, though very thin. You eating?"

"Yes, though not as much as Momma wants me to. I feel good most days, though the Big Sleep almost took me in the doctor's place a couple of moon cycles ago. Momma came to visit me, and I fought to stay alive." Khan rubbed along Black's body, his joy coursing through him. "I know that the Big Sleep is coming soon, but I fight it, because my momma needs me. Some days are very hard because my belly hurts, but when Momma cries, I try to be strong."

"Kid," Black flashed Khan a feline smile, "you have a wonderful momma. Not all cats get such loving human parents."

"I do," Khan purred raggedly. "I will never forget how happy I was to see you escaped the Big Sleep."

"You will escape it this time, too. Never stop the fight. I hope what we talked about so many mooncycles ago is true. I've never seen such a strong bond between momma and cat like you have."

"It's very strong. I only hope strong enough." Khan paused, then asked, "Black, do you know Oliver?"

"Yes. I have met him briefly at the cat doctor's. But I've never spoken to him. Why?"

"He is a wise old cat, and reminds me of you."

"I remember him," Phantom interjected. "When I broke my jaw, he visited me. He didn't stay long because so many of the other cats got upset that he was out and about."

"You didn't react likewise?" Khan teased.

"No. I was too sleepy, but he did peek in at my jaw. It seemed my injury made the gossip around there for a while. He wished me well. Seemed a good sort."

"He is. Like Black," Khan retorted, old anger stirring. "They are both wise and experienced."

"I have learned you were right," Phantom capitulated. "Both are wise in their own ways. Black, even if I seem it, I really mean you no harm anymore. Really."

"Old habits die hard, I know," Black said. "I hope we can be friends, even if only for Khan's sake."

"I promise I won't ever hurt you again."

"I know. We have come to a good agreement. I will always respect your territory, now that I understand your ways."

"I am glad I listened to Khan and sat to talk to you. I will always feel jealous of your friendship," Phantom sighed. "You knew him before I did."

"To be expected, considering that when Khan and I met, you were but a mere tiny kitten. Remember that, and always remember how much he loves you now, and how he did when you met each other. I envy your bond. Never take it for granted."

"I won't. You are my best friend," Khan said, rubbing against Phantom. "You were so scared when we met, but I wanted you to like me so badly."

"I remember. I was a silly kitten."

"I must go now. Enjoy the sun, both of you." Black Satin turned abruptly, and walked across the lawn into Rumple's yard. He leaped on the fence, and balanced on a post, poised like a black statue. He glanced backward.

"Fight the good fight, my old friend," he meowed, before disappearing over the fence around the pool.

"I will always fight this," Khan mewled softly, watching his old friend vanish. He twitched his tail, which curled and flopped in response.

"Momma needs you," Phantom purred. "And so do I."

"I do not want to leave this place, ever," Khan purred back, and glanced up at Momma, then back at Phantom.

"We want you here," Phantom said softly. "So does Black. He doesn't say much, but I know he is worried for you."

"I know," Khan murmured, then shook himself, and broke into a brisk walk, determined to battle this monster inside him. He drank in the warm air, enjoying the scents, relishing the sun on his back. He buried his troubles and pain in the back of his mind, feeling the love from his momma as it traveled down the leash to caress his body.

© *Marie J.S. Phillips*

# CHAPTER 17: RELAPSE

Days later, Khan woke with an upset belly. He walked slowly out of his bed, but ignored the food bowls. He climbed into the litter box, then retched.

"Are you all right?" Phantom called from the food area. Khan turned, and left the litter box, joining Phantom. His momma cleaned the box, chattering her concerns to Poppy.

"My belly is wrestling with itself," Khan answered, and nibbled some dry food. He picked up a large golden piece of kibble, his favorite, and chewed. "Yet, I do feel hungry."

"Feel like playing?"

"No. I'm tired." Khan turned away from the bowl, and sauntered to the livingroom. He took his place on the back of his favorite chair, to look out the window. His belly rumbled, and he felt queasy. He hunched in a ball, trying to ease his discomfort. He dozed until he heard his momma and poppy sit down for midday dinner. He jumped down from the chair, and trotted to the dining room. He reared up, and gently placed his paws on Momma's leg.

"Momma? Momma?" Khan bleated softly. She stroked his head, peering under the table.

"What do you want, sweetie?" she asked, and resumed eating. He circled the table, and reared up on her chair back, tapping her with a gentle paw.

"Momma, my tummy hurts! Help me feel better!"

Momma ran her hand down his spine, and, in her touch, he felt her love and worry.

"I don't know what you want, my Baby Boy," Momma said. Khan placed his paws in her lap, then dropped to the floor, rubbing against her chair, looking back at her.

"My belly hurts," Khan answered with a rattling purr. But she did not understand him. He gave up, and retired to the livingroom, curling on his chair. He snuggled into the pillows. He snoozed, until the urge to throw up woke him. He tried to leap from the chair, but only succeeded in extending his head so the mess missed his favorite sleeping place. Momma came into the room on the run.

"Oh, my poor baby! Come on, let's get you some medicine."

Khan flicked his ears, but did not protest. He hated taking pills or liquids, but let Momma carry him to the kitchen. She gently opened his mouth, and pumped sweet nasty liquid down his throat. He shook his head, unable to help showing how much he hated that medication.

"It's sweet-tasting, baby," Momma said soothingly. "Why do you hate it so much?"

"Nasty," Khan said, but, despite years of all the cats trying to teach her, Momma did not understand much cat-speak. She patted him.

"This will make you feel better," Momma said, and returned to her chores. Khan trotted back into the livingroom, and curled up on the catbed next to the Christmas Tree. He slept. He woke again in the evening, and retched fluid. He sat, miserable, his whole insides battling themselves. The night wore on, and Khan huddled on his cat bed, his stomach twisting and knotting. Phantom sat beside his cage.

"Are you all right?" he asked worriedly. "I smell something wrong again."

"I feel very bad," Khan mumbled. "Very bad."

The next day, while football games played on the television, Khan huddled on his bed. His stomach tortured him, and he threw up more fluid and yellow bile. Momma tried giving him medications, but he retched them all up. He knew she worried, but he felt so terrible he barely registered her attentions. Phantom sat by his cage.

"You smell so wrong. Will you leave like Munchkin did?"

"I don't know," Khan whispered. "Munchkin went to the Big Sleep. I don't want to go to the Big Sleep, but it hurts so much."

Phantom blinked, eyes full and sad, then left the room. That night, prior to lights out, Momma crouched in front of Khan, reaching into his bedcage to hug him and scratch his ears. He purred raggedly. She sobbed.

"Oh, Khan, I love you so much! Please, you can't leave me yet. I can't deal with it." She wept, closed the cage, and went to her bed. In the silence of the night, Khan continued to vomit. The next morning, after cleaning up his messes, Momma took him out of his bedcage. He saw the carrier waiting and open next to his bed, and headed straight for it.

"Cat doctor make me feel better?" Khan asked, as he curled up in the familiar box.

"Oh, good boy! You know, you know, don't you? They will make you feel better."

Khan felt little of his normal fears and apprehension as Momma brought him into the Animal Hospital. He lay in his carrier, purring, unable to muster the strength to feel fear or widen his eyes. Momma noticed.

"You poor baby. You are so sick. They will help you, sweet one."

"Please help me," Khan meowed. "It hurts so much."

After a short wait, Momma carried Khan to the exam room. As the cat doctor and his assistant pulled Khan out, old fears returned, and adrenaline pumped into his limbs. He leaped off the table, but Momma caught him, and placed him back. He breathed heavily, his strength gone. His momma spoke with the cat doctor, and their voices floated around his ears.

Suddenly, his momma hugged him and said, "Be a good boy."

The quaver in her voice alerted him, and, as the nurse carried him away from Momma, he bleated. They gave him several injections, and placed him in a cage. He missed his momma already. Why did she leave? Then, his insides convulsed, and he threw up, forgetting everything but his burning tortured insides.

Nightfall darkened the hospital, and Khan wished to lie down and sleep, to forget the pain, but he remembered his momma's weeping, and fought the darkness threatening to suck him into blissful oblivion. He never wanted to leave her, and watched warily in the deep of night for The Rift. Soft-padded footfalls attracted his attention.

"Sorry to see you so sick," Oliver's voice whispered to him. The old tabby peered up into Khan's cage, and cocked his head. "What were you staring at?"

"The Vortex. I think it's coming for me."

"Not if the Doc and his staff have anything to say about it." Oliver leaped to the table nearest Khan's cage. "They all love you here, you know."

"So? My momma does, too, but she can't stop this sickness."

"But the docs can. Try not to sit and worry about The Vortex. Fight to get well. Eat. You must eat. The Doc will help you. The Vortex won't come for you as long as you fight to live."

"I will try my best. I don't want to leave."

"Good." Oliver jumped to the floor, ignoring the hisses of the patient in the cage beneath Khan's. "They will poke you, handle you, stick you with needles, but its for your own good."

"I'll be brave, for Momma," Khan said, and resolved to not battle the cat nurses.

The next morning, the cat doctor came in, checking his progress with the night nurses, and injected him with shots. He listened, and watched the busy activity of the hospital, spotting Oliver's figure many times as the doors swung open. As night brought quiet to the Animal Hospital, Khan curled up, but listened for familiar paw treads.

"Better this evening?" Oliver asked, slipping into the room. Khan raised his head.

"Yes, a little, but I can't stop the nausea."

"It will pass. You will see." Oliver waved his tail and left. Khan drew comfort from Oliver's confident words. As night turned to dawn, he realized his belly hurt less. He vomited only a few times, and the cat doctors and their technicians smiled at him as they continued to stick him with needles. He endured every last prick without even a hiss or meow of pain. That night, he slept better than the past several nights. He heard Oliver's soft tread on the linoleum, but barely opened one eye. Oliver purred.

"You are resting comfortably tonight, I see."

"Yes," Khan purred back.

"Good! You'll be eating soon. Try. You must eat."

Before Khan inhaled enough air for a reply, Oliver left the room.

The next day, they offered Khan food, but he refused, despite Oliver's words the night before. One of the nurses held him, and gently forced food into him. He swallowed several times, until his belly revolted. He drooled, feeling queasy.

"Stop, stop," he pleaded. "I don't want to be sick again!"

The nurse stopped immediately, as if she understood him. He lay down, and they injected his body again with medication. The food stayed down. That evening, the same cat nurse fed him again, and this time he felt no nausea. His lower abdomen still rumbled, but the pain did not stab so deep. He huddled until the pain subsided, relieved his food stayed down. He warily watched the room, until the soft landing of cat paws interrupted his vigil. Khan turned, and recognized Oliver, who sat on the exam table across the room, looking at him.

"Hello," Khan greeted the grey-brown tabby.

"What has you so nervous in the dark again?"

"The Vortex," Khan murmured, and glanced up at the dark ceiling.

"It can't come for a living cat. I told you, you aren't going to the Big Sleep. That is the only time it comes is when a cat is no longer alive."

"I know, but I fear it might still take me, like it did Mandee. She returned to us as a spirit, and it came back for her."

"Poor girl. I remember her well. Such a pretty female. The doctors tried so hard to make her well, but her body failed." Oliver lashed his tail. "But she disobeyed natural law. You have not."

"You sound like a wise old friend of mine," Khan said, relaxing into his bedding. "Do you know a lot about the Big Sleep?"

"More than I ever wanted to know."

"What about life energies and how they cycle? Can I make sure I can come back to my momma when I do go to the Big Sleep?"

"I have seen such happen, but it is very rare. So many things have to go right, but, most important, if the bond with your momma is not strong enough, you will not be reunited." Oliver flicked his ears, his green eyes thoughtful. "In all instances I have seen, the cat pulled energy from his and his momma's shared love. If your time does come, Big Khan, if your momma loves you like you love her, use that energy. It may not work, but there is no harm in trying."

"Thank you. That gives me some hope."

"Just don't think it will really happen. You may be disappointed. It is a rare thing. Even what your friend Mandee accomplished was so rare, and she never returned after The Vortex took her, did she?"

"No."

"To return as a new kitten, and know it, is near impossible, I think. If that is what you want, I wish you luck, but -- don't get your hopes up." Oliver jumped down, and paused before leaving the room. "Good night, Khan."

"Thanks," Khan mewled in response. He slept well that night, wanting, more than anything, to go home.

© Marie J.S. Phillips

# CHAPTER 18: BACK FROM THE BRINK

Khan woke before the cat nurses arrived in the morning. They offered him food, and he took one sniff, turning his head away. He allowed them to force food into him again, and his belly did not protest. He felt strength returning to his body. His doctor gave him a shot later that day, and his nurse settled in to feed him again. Khan smelled the food, and, this time, it smelled wonderful. He reached down and lapped up the soft food he knew so well. One of his favorites. The cat doctor and his nurses praised him, and all seemed so happy. With all the pain gone, he thought of home.

"Is my momma coming?" he meowed, worrying, yet recalling his last visit when he stayed for many days. Hours later, the nurse came to his cage, a big smile on her face.

"You're going home, Big Boy."

"Home?" Khan bleated, as they placed him in a familiar carrier. Confusion washed through him as the nurse carried his carrier out into the busy waiting area. A face suddenly appeared in front of the grate, and a voice boomed into his ears.

"My sweet one!"

Khan hitched forward on wobbling legs, recognizing the voice and the scent which floated into the carrier.

"Momma! Momma!" he purred strong, and touched his nose to her fingers. He purred the entire ride home, his mind and heart full of joy. Once in the house he loved, Khan walked out of his carrier, wobbling on weak legs, heading for the kitchen. Phantom rushed forward, touching noses. Warlocke joined them. Indy watched from across the room, eyes wide.

"You were gone so long! You don't smell wrong anymore!" Phantom purred his joy.

"I am tired, and weak, but my belly is much better," Khan explained. "I am hungry."

Khan settled beside the food bowls, and ate the dry kibble. All that evening, his lower belly rumbled and sometimes hurt, but not with stabbing pains. The next morning, Momma took him gently in her grasp, pulled out cans of oily food, and, to his surprise, fastened a small piece of cloth around his neck. He tried stepping out of it, but failed. Momma chuckled.

"Aww, baby, keep the bib on. It keeps your chest clean. Until you take all your food without spitting some out, you have to wear it," Momma admonished. "And you must wear it when you take your chemo, sweetie."

Khan pawed at the white terry cloth with the pink writing. Food spilled from his chin, and Momma smiled.

"See? You need it, little slob. It says, 'I love my Mommy.' You look so cute in it."

Khan swallowed the last serving, as Momma put away the syringes. Phantom walked into the kitchen, and sneezed feline mirth.

"What is that thing anyway? How undignified."

"Don't laugh. If Momma fussed over you and made you wear it, you wouldn't fight her either." Khan licked his lips as Momma removed the bib.

"I'd never wear that," Indy meowed in derision, trotting quickly past him. "I'd claw and bite."

"You're a fool to hurt Momma," Khan retorted. "She just loves me, and wants me to feel better."

"It does look funny," Warlocke said, his face a feline smile. "I don't know if I'd wear it either, but I'd never claw Momma."

Khan accepted the bib, despite his housemates' teasing. It did not hurt in any way, and Momma fussed over him when he wore it. The medications and oily rich food began to work. The next day, after his medication, his appetite returned in a rush, urging him to eat. He sampled every food, canned and dry, Momma offered him. He spent more time in the kitchen than anywhere else in the house. Later that day, Momma wrapped Christmas gifts, talking with Poppy, her tone happy. Khan jumped up on the chair behind her, and settled on his belly, purring. Momma turned and laughed.

"You're gonna help me wrap presents, Baby?"

Sudden pressure in Khan's lower belly surprised him, and, before he knew it, a short sharp noise exploded behind him. His purr rose with shock, and he leaped from the chair, looking behind him.

"What was that?"

"You passed gas," Phantom purred in mirth. "Feels good, doesn't it? Humans find it very funny."

"Ugh!" Momma suddenly exclaimed. "Who is farting?"

She turned, and looked down at Khan, and broke up laughing.

"You! You did that! Oh, my God! You are stinking us out of the house!"

Khan sat down, and purred, blinking at Momma, and realized his lower belly felt better. All that evening, expulsion of gas from his behind surprised him with the noise, and earned him uproarious laughter from both Momma and Poppy, who thought it all very funny, just as Phantom predicted earlier. Khan grew used to the experience, and, with each episode, he felt immeasurably better.

The next day, the gaseous explosions stopped, and Khan reveled in the strength and energy returning to his weak, boney body. He joined Phantom in play, and wrestled with Warlocke, but tired quickly. He enjoyed every bite of his food. Momma hugged him often, her joy evident. Khan dutifully accepted all force-fed offerings and medications while wearing his bib.

"My skinny pot-bellied boy," she teased, caressing his stuffed abdomen, then his emaciated hips. "Now you must put what is in here, up here."

"I am trying, Momma! I want to be strong for you. I want to fight this wrongness that keeps coming back," Khan purred. Momma returned to her work, and Khan walked to the food bowls, wishing his momma understood him. Sometimes, it seemed like she did, but most of the time, his talk never registered with her.

One morning, Momma picked up Khan, and placed him in the carrier.

"No, Momma! I feel good! I don't want to go to the doctor!"

"Be a good boy, baby," Momma said in reassurance. "You need to go for your check-up. And they have a new medicine for you. It will make you feel even better."

Khan protested with an inarticulate meow.

"You want to feel all better, right? So Momma doesn't worry about you when Poppy and I go to visit my mama?"

Khan gazed up at her, remembering the few times a year Momma and Poppy left for a few days. The friendly neighbor woman and her son, or the neighbor man, always came to make sure he and his housemates received food, water, and treats. Though Khan missed his momma and poppy at these times, he enjoyed this special time with his other human friends. He purred.

"I'll try to be good," he mewed. "I want to feel even better."

He tried to fight his normal anxieties about going to the cat doctor, but old habits died hard. In the waiting area, he huddled in the back of his carrier, eyes wide, and Momma peeked in at him.

"I see you are back to normal."

Khan blinked, and uttered one ragged purr. Once in the exam room, Khan protested as the doctor and Momma extricated him from the carrier. After the doctor checked him over, Momma hugged him.

"Be a good boy." To his surprise, the doctor brought him in back, and placed him into a cage. He bleated.

"Momma!"

The doctor and his assistants shaved his belly, and stuck him with needles. He wiggled, but remembered Momma's words. He tried to behave, as the doctor carefully stuck a long needle into his shaved abdomen. Khan endured it, wide-eyed and scared. They placed him in a cage, and kept checking on him. He wondered what they expected to happen to him. He waited patiently, knowing from experience that his momma would come and pick him up. Sure enough, near dusk, Momma arrived to bring Khan home. Khan listened as the doctor told Momma how well he behaved. Khan felt proud of himself, and purred during the ride. Momma chattered happily, exclaiming as she admired all the holiday decorations. Khan peered from the carrier, catching sight of some of the sparkling lights.

Once home, he emerged from the carrier. Phantom trotted up to him.

"What did they do this time?"

"They gave me a big needle. Doctor called it Elspar. It's a cancer medicine, I think," Khan replied.

"Are you hungry?"

"Yes," Khan answered. He followed Phantom to the food bowls, well aware of Momma's joy in his progress. He hoped his full strength returned soon. He hated feeling weak and sick.

## CHAPTER 19: NEW YEAR'S JOY

The day of Momma and Poppy's trip arrived swiftly. Khan watched them bustle around as they packed the car.

"I will miss Momma. Poppy, too," he lamented.

"So will I," Phantom grumbled, then brightened. "But we will have the whole house to play in!"

"Yes, that is always fun. I like when Auntie and her son come to feed and play with us. Why do you hide?"

"I don't know. Can't help it."

"I hide, too," Warlocke said, joining the group as the door closed for the final time. "But I eventually come out. It's hard getting used to new things or humans."

"Silly," Khan meowed. "There is nothing to fear."

"One can never be too cautious," Phantom said, and walked away. Khan followed, and, as usual, Phantom stopped at the food bowl.

"Always eating," Khan teased his best buddy. Phantom lifted his head, swallowing.

"Ha! You could do with some chowing down. You aren't gaining weight back."

"I know." Khan sat in front of his kibble bowl. "But I eat well many days. I gain some, lose it again. It's the sickness."

That evening, the front door opened. Phantom, Warlocke, and Indy scattered to hide. Khan watched them as he sauntered down the hall.

"Silly cats," he said.

The neighbor and her son greeted Khan with affectionate pats on the head. They fussed over him as they put the food on the floor. Khan purred and ate, pleasing his caretakers. Once they left, his housemates came out of the shadows to eat. Phantom scooped up mouthfuls of kibble, flinging his head back, scattering food as he tried to gulp down as much as possible.

"Glutton," Khan teased. "You drop more than you can hold."

"I'm hungry," Phantom mumbled around his food. Khan smirked, and drank water.

Two days passed quickly and Khan enjoyed the attentions of Auntie and her young son. On the third day, his caretakers did not show up in the morning. The door opened that afternoon and, Momma and Poppy walked in. Khan greeted them with his customary delight, and Momma picked him up and hugged him.

"Did you miss us?"

"Of course," Khan purred strong into Momma's ear.

The next morning, Khan woke up with a stuffy head. He heard Poppy coming down the stairs. He sat up in his bed and yawned, waiting for Momma to walk into the room. She came down right after Poppy, and let Khan out of his bed cage. She carefully inspected his litterbox, and praised him when she noticed the empty food dishes.

As the day progressed, so did Khan's cat cold. His nose ran, and the stuff dripped down the back of his throat. Gagging on the phlegm, he vomited an hour after Momma gave him his very important pill. Momma searched for the pill, and Khan watched as she prodded his regurgitated food with a gloved finger. She finally tossed it in a plastic bag and threw it away, but she gave him worried glances all day. Khan purred when she picked him up for a hug.

"Don't let a runny nose stop you from eating," Phantom said, when Momma put him down after a hug.

"But I can't smell the food," Khan protested.

"So?" Phantom sneezed suddenly. "We all have this silly cold. How can you not eat?"

"Water runs from my nose," Khan grumbled.

"So? Eat. You have to be hungry."

"I am."

"Then come on. Eat with me." Phantom gazed at him, sea-green eyes full of concern. "You are getting thinner again. Please, eat, and make Momma happy."

Khan followed his buddy to the food bowls, and nibbled on his kitten food. Phantom gobbled his share down greedily. Khan twitched his tail, and dutifully ate his supper.

A few days later, at the cat doctor's, Khan received more shots. He endured them, hoping to feel better, as he always did after his shots. As usual, they helped. The next evening, he sat in front of his kibble bowl and eagerly ate. Phantom joined him.

"About time! You should always eat like that."

"Yeah," Khan replied, taking another big piece of dry food into his jaws. "It makes Momma so happy. But sometimes I can't help it."

"I know," Phantom said softly, and resumed his attack on his soft food. Khan uttered a soft meow, and returned to eating. He felt the disease churning inside him, and fought with every bit of strength he possessed. Instinct told him the war with this internal monster wasted energy and time. The cancer lost battles, but slowly won the war within him, and he knew it, but he felt he must fight, for his momma. He nibbled his food even after he felt full. Momma and Poppy puttered about the kitchen, preparing treats for New Year's Eve. Phantom followed each of them, meowing his delight. He inhaled any tidbit they dropped during the preparations.

"They aren't gonna give you that food," Khan said, leaving the food bowls. Phantom followed. Khan and Phantom walked into the livingroom, where Momma and Poppy sat. Plates of special human food spread out on the coffee table. Warlocke lay next to the Christmas tree, interested in the boxes. Phantom sniffed the air.

"Such wonderful things!"

"You are not allowed to have them," Khan warned.

"Sometimes Momma gives me samples," Phantom retorted.

"Not since you stole her Christmas cookie off the table last year," Khan reminded him.

"Three, two, ONE!" Both Momma's and Poppy's chants startled Khan. Momma suddenly scooped him up, as she and Poppy cried "Happy New Year!" and, embracing each other, hugged Khan between them. Khan broke into surprised purring.

"Happy New Year, Khan," Poppy said, stroking Khan's head.

"You made it, sweet baby! You made it to 2002!" Momma said in his ear. Khan purred louder, knowing, somehow, he pleased Momma very much.

"Momma is so happy," Phantom meowed from the floor. Khan looked down.

"I made it into the next suncycle," Khan mewed. "I think Momma did not think I would."

"I know she did not," Phantom said, then lowered his voice. "Nor did I."

"Nor did we," Warlocke and Indy said in unison from beside the Christmas tree.

"This cancer monster is trying to eat me up, but," Khan paused, flattening his ears in defiance, "I won't let it win without the battle of my life."

As if she understood him, Khan's Momma hugged him tighter, and a human tear dropped on his head. He turned his head to meet his Momma's tear-filled eyes, and purred loud and strong.

"I am strong," Khan meowed with pride. "I'll fight to be with my Momma, always, because I am a Maine Coon!"

© Marie J. S. Phillips

# CHAPTER 20: THE CHEMO NEEDLES

Cold winter winds moaned in the eaves, driving snow against the windows. Khan lay in his bedcage, listening, snuggled on his bed. His stomach rumbled, and he inhaled, letting it out in a growling sigh. Phantom appeared beside his bed, padding on silent paws.

"You feeling ill again?" Worry colored Phantom's soft meow.

"Yes, a little. I hate having the watery poop. It's back again." Khan turned to face his friend. "Momma

171

put the carrier down on the floor. I am probably going to the cat doctor again tomorrow."

"They will make you better. They always do," Phantom said, then slanted back his ears. "But it's always so scary there."

"I know." Khan yawned. "I used to be so scared, but now, I just get nervous."

"I smell something wrong, but it is not real bad," Phantom said, poking his nose against the gilded bars.

"I do not feel real sick, but I hate the watery poop." Khan grimaced in disdain, flicking his ears. "Then Momma cuts my britches off."

"She did a long time ago. They aren't growing back."

"I know." Khan sighed, and curled up. Phantom left him, and sauntered into the kitchen. Khan listened to his buddy chow down on dry kibble. Khan ignored his food, not wanting to vomit on his nice clean bed. He dozed off, and slept, until he heard Poppy come down the stairs. He opened his eyes. Early dawn light brightened the large windows. Fresh snow blanketed the outdoors, brightening up the world. Khan purred as Poppy walked by.

"Morning, Khan," Poppy greeted him, glancing down at him on the way to the bathroom. "Mommy will be happy to hear that purr."

Momma came down a little while later, and stopped by Khan's cage. She opened the door.

"Morning, sweet one. Oh, my, you did not eat much, did you?"

"Sorry, Momma," Khan purred, stretching as he walked out of his bedcage. He walked to the food bowls, and sniffed.

"Nothing smells good," he said, and sat down.

"Poor baby. You will eat better soon. The doctor is going to give you new medicines," Momma said, pouring coffee.

"I knew it," Khan said, glancing at Phantom. "I am going to the doctor again."

"I hope it's not too scary," Phantom said between swallows.

"Me, too." Warlocke's voice joined them as he entered the room, greeting Momma with a high-pitched meow. Warlocke stopped at the food bowl, and ate. The young Maine Coon's bushy silver-touched black tail twitched to and fro.

"You should eat," he said, glancing at Khan. "Momma put down your favorite nuggets. I love them, too."

"I love them, but I just don't feel like eating any." Khan watched his buddies eat, then left the kitchen. He entered the darkened livingroom and jumped up on a chair. He snuggled in the pillows, and waited.

A few hours later, after the sun's rays brightened the room, Momma came into the room. She lifted Khan, and brought him to the carrier. Khan resisted.

"No, Momma!"

"Come on, honey bear, get in. You know you have to get your medicines."

Khan relented, and let Momma push him into the box. He uttered a few bleats of protest, but knew nothing stopped visits to the cat doctor. As Momma secured his carrier with the seat belt, he settled down. Once they arrived at the Animal Hospital, Khan's nervousness returned. He meowed softly as Momma placed him on the bench. A cat nurse walked over and called Khan's name. Momma stood up, grasping his carrier, and followed the tech into one of the exam rooms. Khan's heart jumped, beating faster.

"Nooo!" he mewled. "I don't want to stay. Momma!"

The nurse gently pulled him out of the carrier, brought him to the back, and placed him on the scale. He stood still, knowing this part of the procedure well. The tech carried him back to Momma, and said, "Ten point seven."

"Oh, no," Momma responded, alarm in her voice. "He's under eleven pounds again."

"Hopefully, the new chemo will help," the nurse said. "Say goodbye for now."

"Be a good boy for the doctor, sweet one," Momma said, and left the room.

"Mooommmaaa!" Khan wailed. The cat nurse stroked his head.

"It's OK, Khan. We will be gentle, Big Guy."

Khan knew all of the people here loved him, but he always feared what came next. They shaved one of his front legs, and he struggled not to bolt as they drew blood. He concentrated on the memory of Oliver's words to him during his last stay at the hospital. The doctor and his techs spoke softly to him, trying to reassure him. Khan lay quiet, knowing the drill, and tried to calm his racing heart. He must be strong for Momma! They left him alone a while, and he began to relax in the cage. He sniffed the bars, and inspected the now-familiar spartan interior.

"My bedcage is better," he remarked.

"You have a cage at home?" A cat in the next cage growled. Khan glanced at the budding tomcat. Always friendly to strangers, he put his whiskers forward and flicked his tail in greeting.

"Yes. My momma puts me in at it night."

"Why?" The young cat clawed the bars of his cage. "Your momma?"

"My momma, a human. She keeps me safe there. My housemates can't steal my food or use my litterbox. Momma needs to know if I eat and use the box."

"No human would dare do that to me. I'm not a silly human child."

"No human?" Khan asked, surprised by the cat's tone. "You don't have a human momma?"

"I have a human that gives me what I need -- food, a place to sleep, but otherwise I do as I please."

"You don't love your momma? You don't live inside with your momma and poppy?"

"I don't know what you mean," the cat sneered. "You are a baby, one of those pampered ones who have no freedoms. You even look different, too."

"I am a Maine Coon," Khan growled in retort. Memory flooded Khan, as he recalled the cranky female who hated him for no reason many years ago in the shelter. Khan slanted back his ears, feeling not like a shamed kitten, but an indignant proud cat. "I'd rather be with my momma than alone on the streets, or ignored. Your human just feeds you, and then ignores you. You don't know love. I bet your human never hugs you or pets you."

"I don't want them touching me," the cat spat, its white, grey-spotted fur rising. "They grabbed me this morning, and brought me here. I don't know why, but I am so mad at them. I may leave."

"You are stupid then, worse than my housemate Indy is." Khan sat up to his full height, ignoring any discomfort. "You have never loved or been loved by a human momma. Until you have, you will be unhappy. At least Indy loves in his own way. Even he knows what you don't."

"I'm not unhappy, but I'd be happier out of here," the cat snarled. "You're just a pampered coddled baby."

"If so, so be it," Khan growled back, standing up to his full height, puffing out his long hair. He glared balefully at the other, ears back, showing his sudden anger. "You don't know true happiness and joy in love. If not for such coddling, as you put it, I'd have gone to the Big Sleep long ago. My momma loves me, and I love her, so I battle this disease that eats me up. If you catch a bad sickness, and have no loving momma, you'll go to the Big Sleep alone, in pain, and scared."

"I'm not going to the Big Sleep! Leave me alone!" the young tom hissed, and backed up against the opposite wall of his cage. Khan smelled the stranger's sudden fear of him, and puffed out his thinning coat.

"You started this," Khan growled, aware of human footfalls in the room.

"Whoa, Big Guy!" the doctor said in surprise, opening Khan's cage, stopping the vocal war. "What is wrong? You're scaring that little tomcat."

"He's young and dumb," Khan protested, as the doctor took him back to the exam table, placing him on the cool metal. Khan forgot the ornery cat as the doctor barked out crisp orders. The techs hurried to obey him. Khan tensed. Something seemed very different this time. The doctor took Khan's leg, and, speaking softly, gently inserted a strange needle into his leg. Khan watched, his eyes widening.

"What is this?" he meowed.

The doctor smiled at him, as if he understood.

"It's OK, Big Guy, it's OK. Just stay still, and it will be over fast."

With great care, the doctor inserted another needle into the strange contraption stuck in his leg, then injected a small amount of liquid. Khan dared not move, afraid the weird sensation might turn painful if he even twitched. In minutes, the procedure ended, and the tech placed Khan back in his cage. He looked into the next cage, but saw no young tom. Khan laid down and purred, hoping Momma soon arrived to bring him home.

To his surprise, Oliver strolled into the room.

"Oliver!"

"Hello, Khan." Oliver stopped, and sat down. "All going well?"

"Yes," Khan slanted back his ears. "But I have a question."

"What?"

"Do you think I am a coddled pampered baby?"

"No. What gave you that idea?"

Khan relayed his angry conversation with the crabby grey-spotted tom earlier. Oliver flattened his ears briefly.

"He was a young fool who has never known a good home. We are the lucky ones." Oliver stood up, tail in the air. "Be so thankful you have a loving human momma. Many don't. That cruel young one knows nothing. Don't ever fret over this again."

"I won't," Khan purred.

"I am so glad to see you feeling better," Oliver said. His eyes slitted in a mischievous feline grin. "I know where the tomcat is. I think I'll have a nice talk with the poor young one when he comes back."

"He'll be back here?"

"Yes. He is undergoing his neutering," Oliver answered. "I hope you are still here when he wakes up, but even if you aren't, this will be fun."

"What will you do?"

"A good old-fashioned hissing battle. That young one needs to respect his elders," Oliver chuckled low in his chest, then sauntered back out to the reception area. Khan relaxed, watching the empty cage beside him. A cat nurse returned the young cat to his cage, but he lay still, under the influence of the anesthesia. Khan watched him, but he never woke up. Khan tired of watching the cranky cat sleep, so he waited for the arrival of his momma. When the sun hit its zenith, a cat nurse opened his cage. In the next cage, the young neutered cat stirred.

"What happened to me?" he croaked, terror in his weak voice. As the cat nurse carried Khan away, he called out.

"Don't be afraid. Oliver will explain things to you."

"Hello, my sweet bear!" The loved voice drove thoughts of the young cat from Khan's mind.

"Momma!" he bleated, as the cat nurse gently urged him into his familiar carrier. Joy coursed through him as Momma carried him to the car, and drove him home.

Khan returned the following week for another procedure, the same as the last. He returned every week for the same treatment, but never saw the angry young cat again. With each passing week, he felt stronger. His appetite returned, making his momma happy. The weather warmed one day, and Momma opened the windows. Excitement flowed through Khan. He joined Warlocke and Indy on the chair back, inhaling the early spring scents wafting in the window. He jostled Indy in an attempt for a better view, and, to his surprise, Indy merely flicked an ear. Warlocke sat beside him on his other side, alert, not caring if Khan leaned into him.

"This is so wonderful," Khan said. "Maybe Momma will take me outside?"

"Maybe," Warlocke replied. "I'd rather sit right here. Too scary out there."

"No, it isn't," Khan admonished. "You had one bad thing happen, when the bee stung you, and now you're scared silly."

"I know. I can't help it."

Khan twitched his tail, and returned his attention to the glorious sunbathed day beyond the screen. The next morning, as Khan ate his breakfast, Phantom sniffed him.

"The bad scent is fading."

"It is?"

"Yes. This medicine is working." Phantom cocked his head. "Does it hurt when they give it to you?"

"Very little," Khan answered. "As long as I stay still."

"I am glad. Your first time, I thought you were upset by it. You seemed angry that day."

"Oh, it wasn't the treatment, or you, but some dumb young cat I met."

"What did he do?"

"He called me a coddled baby." Khan lifted his head from his food. "He said he didn't need or want a human momma, that he came and went as he pleased.

He had a human who fed him and let him stay sheltered in bad weather, but he did not live inside with them."

"He sounds like a poor luckless stray to me. If Munchkin were still here, he'd tell you that kind of life lacks love."

"The cat didn't care about that." Khan lashed his tail. "Is something wrong with us?"

"No!" Phantom spat, flattening his ears. "Remember Munchkin's first days? How desperate he was to get inside? He wanted a human momma to love. Maybe this cat never knew the love of human mommas and poppas, so he has no idea what he is missing. Ask Black or Oliver about it. I'll bet they have enough to say on the subject."

"Yes, you're right. Oliver already told me the cat was young and foolish, but it did get me angry." Khan returned to his meal, and put the stranger out of his mind. Khan ate with vigor, but, try as he might, his body refused to gain the weight he needed so much.

©2002 Marie J. S. Phillips

## 21: INDIGNITIES

Khan lay on the metal table, allowing the doctor to administer the last dose of his treatment. For two mooncycles, he felt good, and ate. The pressure inside him eased its onslaught for a while. He even gained some weight, pleasing Momma and the doctor, but the doctor now watched him with a worried frown. Khan knew why. Lost weight, and bouts of the watery poops, not to mention the disgusting vomiting, plagued him this past week. The doctor finished, then placed Khan in his cage to await his momma.

Momma arrived, and, as the doctor spoke to her, Khan heard the worry in both voices.

"His left kidney is enlarged," the doctor said, following Momma out of the exam room. "I fear the lymphoma has spread, despite the chemo."

"What can we do?" Momma asked, her voice shaking.

"Switch his chemo protocol again, and see if we can't arrest the growth."

"Whatever he needs," Momma answered. Khan wondered what else he might have to deal with. He uttered a growly sigh as Momma carried him to the car. Once home, he quickly exited the box. Phantom met him, sniffing his nose, then his body.

"It's back, isn't it? I knew I smelled it again."

"Yes, it is. Momma has new medicines," Khan said, hope in his voice and heart. He never wanted to leave his momma. "I have to go for another shot in my belly."

"Does it hurt?"

"A little, but not bad. The doctor is very gentle."

"I hope this works," Phantom said, flicking his tail. "This time, it smells stronger, different. I am scared for you."

Khan shook himself, and headed for the food bowl. The shot he received worked to make him hungry. Momma force-fed him the oily, funny-tasting food, placing all his pills in it. Khan dutifully ate, but his appetite dwindled as the days warmed and the birds sang outside. One morning, he found it difficult to poop, and he did not know what to do when it stuck half-way out. Phantom sat, watching.

"You have the pasty doots. Scooch it off. Then the rest comes out."

"No!" Khan glared at his best friend. "Momma HATES when you do that. I'll never ever do that. It's disgusting!"

Momma saw him, and brought him into the bathroom. There, she tried with gentle hands to remove the stuck poo. She failed. After Khan tried to use the litterbox several times, Momma scooped him up, and whisked him up to the cat doctor. The doctor gently palpitated Khan's belly, and pain caused him to growl at the doctor. Suddenly, the doctor donned a glove, and stuck his finger in Khan's most private place. Khan uttered a wail of outrage as the doctor removed the offending feces. Khan breathed heavily, and dashed for the safety of his carrier. Momma talked to him all the way home, but he barely heard her. Once home, he crept from the carrier into his bedcage and lay down. Phantom greeted him, his sea-green eyes full of concern.

"What is wrong?"

"You will never believe what the doctor did to me!"

"What?"

Khan told him, and Phantom's eyes dilated with alarm. Indy walked by, paused, and looked back. The bicolor Maine Coon's tail bushed out, and he slanted his ears back.

"And you wonder why I go nuts when anyone touches me, even Momma," he grumbled, then continued out to the food bowls. Khan lay for many hours, until finally his outrage passed, and his tummy felt better. He sauntered to the bowls, and ate a good dinner, pleasing Momma.

A few days later, he suffered the same problem with sticky hard poops. As he entered and re-entered the potty box, Momma scooped him up, and brought him into the bathroom. When she closed the door, Khan looked up at her, eyes wide.

"Nooo! No bath!"

"It's OK, baby," Momma murmured, and knelt down. To Khan's utter shock, she raised his tail, and pushed a slippery cold thing up his rear. He uttered a growling meow in outrage.

"Mooommmmaaa! What are you doing?"

"There, all done. So sorry, baby. But it will help you."

Khan ran from the room, and huddled in his bedcage, ears back, but, in mere minutes, he needed to use the potty box. He rushed in, and, in relief, passed all his stool. He dug furiously, burying it, finding great joy in flinging litter against the walls of the box. Momma praised him, and he felt such delight in his relief that he purred loud and strong, forgetting the indignity which brought about such results.

All went well for a number of days, until the stools began backing up in Khan's belly again. He strained to pass them, but managed only a small pellet or two. Momma worried, and, again, took him to the doctor, who brought him in back to the familiar table, and then, with a gloved hand, cleaned out the stuck doodies.

"Damn," the doctor said to his tech. "Hold him steady. I found something blocking him."

Khan wailed as the doctor reached in, removing the partial blockage. His intestines cramped as the rest of his waste emptied. Khan wailed, heaving for breath, scared and exhausted. The doctor took him back to his momma, and he darted back into the carrier, eyes wide with distress. On the ride home, Momma apologized over and over, reassuring him, but Khan's insides protested with spasms. Once back home, he left the carrier, and lay in his bedcage. Phantom walked over to him, tail above his back.

"What happened?" he asked.

"Bad things," Khan growled. "I don't want to talk about it. My stomach hurts."

"I wish I could make you feel better," Phantom purred softly.

"I know." Khan returned the purr, blinking at his pal. "So does Momma."

In a few days, Khan felt better, and began to eat again. The new medication Momma made him take worked. The shots she gave him stopped his stomach from churning, and he ceased vomiting, much to his relief. He hated throwing up. It hurt so much.

One evening, Momma picked Khan up, and placed him on the dining room table. Alarm shot through him.

"Momma! I'm not allowed up here. What are you doing?" he bleated.

"It's OK, sweetie. You need water.

"I drink a lot of water," Khan protested, but neither Momma nor Poppy heeded his protest. As Poppy gently held him still, Momma inserted a large needle under the skin of his shoulders. Liquid flowed from the needle into his body, running down his shoulder and leg to pool under his belly. The warmth relaxed him, and he wondered why the doctor's treatments to him like this always ran cold. In a few minutes, Momma removed the needle, then gently lowered Khan to the floor. Khan felt the water sloshing under his belly skin, but did not mind. He always felt better after receiving the water needles. He walked into the kitchen, and nibbled his favorite kibble, the big golden nuggets. He chewed, and pain lanced up his tongue. He swallowed, and tried picking up another piece.

"Oww," he said, and lay down in front of the bowl.

"What is wrong?" Warlocke asked, picking his head up from a bowl of soft food.

"My tongue hurts," Khan answered, eyeing the food wistfully. He yawned, showing Phantom.

"Ugh! You have a sore on your tongue."

"It hurts," Khan meowed softly. "Something else to hurt."

Khan rose to his feet, and walked out of the room. He entered the livingroom, and huddled on the rug. Momma picked him up shortly afterward, and gave him his pill with that oily food he did not like. He swallowed it dutifully.

To his relief, as afternoon turned into evening, he felt better. He summoned up his energy, sneezed, and sauntered back into the kitchen. He ate with gusto, ignoring the dull pain on his tongue. Phantom joined him.

"Good to see you eat like that. Momma is so happy."

"I know." Khan paused in his eating. "But I only feel better after that pill. It wears off by morning."

"At least you can eat, and you're not throwing up so much now." Phantom took a bite of food, swallowed, and continued. "But you are getting thinner."

"I know. Nothing seems to help me gain weight. I want to be strong for Momma, but the pressure inside gets worse every day. And the cold won't leave me. It's getting bad again. This sore hurts bad when the pills wear off."

"We all have that stupid cold. You are trying. It is all you can do." Phantom returned to his dinner, and ceased talking. Khan finished his supper, and returned to the livingroom. He jumped up on Momma's lap, and gently kneaded her. He lost strength after a few paw motions, and snuggled into the soft blanket. Momma stroked his bony back, and spoke softly to him. He heard the worry in her tones, and wished he possessed the power to make her happy again.

# CHAPTER 22: BODY BETRAYAL

Days later, the cat doctor placed Khan back on the exam table, after taking blood from him. His stomach churned, and mucus plugged his nose. He barely paid attention to what the doctor told Momma. He just wanted to go home.

In the car, he waited patiently while Momma ran an errand. She returned, carrying a small bag, and spoke to him as she started up the car. Khan's belly protested. To his disgust, he felt the urge to throw up. He sat up in the carrier, and retched. Momma glanced down.

"Oh, no, honey bear, we are almost home!"

Khan heard the telltale sand under the tires, and, as the car swung into the driveway, he lost all control. He gakked as Momma stopped the car, launching the contents of his stomach onto his towel, and out onto the gearshift. Quickly, Momma got out of the car, grabbed his crate, and carried him into the house. She let him out, gave him a quick hug, and hurried back to the car. Khan watched, feeling chagrined that he created a mess in the car.

"What happened?" Phantom asked, hurrying up to him. He sniffed. "You threw up?"

"Yes, in the car. I have never done that before, never."

"Momma understands."

"I know, but I never do that," Khan lamented, and went into the livingroom. He huddled in the patch of sunlight on the rug. Momma returned, and gave him soothing strokes of her hand. He purred raggedly. Momma left him to go back to her work, and he heard her sit in the chair by the computer. He rested, trying to ignore the inner pressure that nauseated him.

Suddenly, Indy waltzed into the room. He stared, then headed to Khan, his face full of mischief.

"You can't do anything to me," he said, and smacked Khan on the back.

"Why are you doing this?" Khan hissed.

"Fun! You can't get me back," Indy chirped, and slapped him again. A sudden low growl echoed in the room, followed by a hiss of anger.

"But I can!" Phantom launched his furry bulk at Indy, slapping him hard several times. Indy hissed and wailed in outrage.

"Don't touch me!"

"Then leave my buddy alone!" Phantom hissed back, chasing Indy across the room. "I'll hurt you if I see you do that again!"

Indy grumbled, and raced upstairs. Both Phantom and Warlocke walked to Khan's side.

"Are you all right?" Warlocke asked in his high-pitched meow.

"Yes, he did not really hurt me."

"But he will, in time," Phantom replied, his eyes still baleful. "Not while I breathe will he hurt you, and harass you like he did poor Mandee and Munchkin."

Khan purred his gratitude.

The next morning, he woke feeling awful. His eyes blurred with mucus, his nose ran, and he refused to leave his bedcage when Momma opened it. Momma pulled him out for his shots, his water needle, his pills, but, after each treatment, he returned to his bedcage and huddled on his soft bed. In the evening, she gently urged him out, and gave him extra pills.

"This will make you feel better," she said. He swallowed the food, then went back to his bed. He heard worry and grief in Momma's words and voice. She cried, holding him before she went to bed. He curled up on the bedding, and wondered about the Big Sleep. He shuddered, remembering Black's words.

"No, no," he whimpered. "I can't leave my momma."

"You all right?" Phantom's question erupted from the dark room.

"No, I am not. My nose is clogged, my eyes are full of stuff, and my belly hurts. The pressure is turning painful."

Phantom appeared out of the shadows, and pressed his nose against the bars. He uttered a sad wail.

"You smell so wrong now. I am scared for you."

"I'm scared, too." Khan curled up. Phantom lay down next to the cage. Khan fell asleep with his buddy's scent trickling up clogged sinuses.

Khan woke the next day, and sat up in surprise. His head felt better, and he scented the air. Phantom entered the room on swift paws.

"You're awake!"

"Yes, and I feel better."

"Go!" Phantom whirled, facing Warlocke, who lay on one of the dining room chairs. "Go wake Momma!"

Warlocke bolted, racing up the stairs, meowing in his high-pitched voice, leaving a wake of black and silver hair behind him. In minutes, Poppy came down the stairs, followed by Momma, who walked behind Warlocke. Momma stopped at Khan's bedcage, and Khan met her gaze, purring.

"Oh, my sweet baby! You feel better?"

In joy, Momma opened the door. Khan walked out, surprised by his shaking legs, but purred loud and strong. He headed for the food bowls, ignoring Momma as she took his private bowls from his cage.

"You ate some dinner overnight? Good boy!"

"You ate last night?" Phantom asked eagerly, awaiting his breakfast. Momma placed the bowls of soft food on the floor.

"Yes, when it began to get light out. I woke up feeling hungry," Khan answered, and turned to his dish. Phantom purred joyously as he ate. Momma prattled on, eating breakfast with Poppy. Khan enjoyed the entire day, breathing through his cleared nasal passages.

The next morning, Khan still felt better, though pressure increased inside him. He staggered leaving his bedcage, and Indy peered at him from under the table. Phantom, always there when Momma opened the bedcage each day, turned his head, glaring at Indy.

"Do not even think about it. How can you bother him like that? He was always good to you, even in your bratty kitten days."

"He's still a brat," Khan added, then turned away from Indy. Though he never showed it, he disliked how Indy upset Momma.

"Indy! You little idiot!!" Momma yelled suddenly. Khan walked to the food area, mincing across the wet floor. He settled in front of the water dish, which now rested in the middle of the flooded linoleum. Khan stared at the empty bowl, then at Indy, who walked into the kitchen to eat. Momma knelt in the feeding area, mopping up water, cursing, glaring at Indy.

"You made Momma mad again. Why must you and Warlocke mess up the water?" Khan growled. "You're the worst! This is such a mess. Now I have to drink this dirty water."

Before Khan took a lap, Momma lifted the bowl, then returned it to the floor, filled with clean cool water. Khan eagerly lapped up the water. Indy uttered a retorting meow, and ran from the room, muttering.

"Brat," Khan called after him.

As the day turned to evening, and Momma and Poppy settled in for relaxation, Khan hurried to the livingroom. Though his legs shook with fatigue, he leaped with great effort into Momma's chair. He settled on the blanket, too tired to knead, and, as she stroked his thin fur, he napped, comforted by her loving touch.

# CHAPTER 23: SPRING SPIRIT

The next morning dawned sunny and warm. Khan stumbled out of his bedcage, shocked by the weakness in his rear legs. His feet slid on the linoleum, and Momma reacted with alarm.

"Oh, my poor sweetie." Momma picked him up, hugged him. Her voice quavered. "You're getting so weak."

"Momma, I'm being as strong as I can. Don't worry," he purred. She put him down as Phantom entered the room.

"You're lucky she doesn't understand our talk," Phantom said. "She'd know you're lying."

"I am trying!" Khan protested. He walked to the food bowls, his feet slipping.

"I know, but you're not getting stronger." Phantom exhaled in a sad mew. "I smell the badness. It grows."

Before Khan replied, Phantom whirled and raced for the front door, meowing stridently. Momma complied with his demand, and let him out. Khan lay down in front of the water bowl, and heaved a big sigh. He heard Momma go outside, forced himself to his feet, and walked slowly down the hall. Momma came in from outdoors, saw him, and held the door open. Khan watched, in shock and surprise.

"Come on, honey bear, you can go out. It's so nice."

Hesitantly, Khan stepped out onto the cement porch, feeling naked without his red harness. Momma chuckled.

"Come on, baby."

Khan walked out, his feet gaining a better grip on the rough surface. He sniffed the air, drinking in all the scents. He carefully made his way off the porch and onto the green lawn. He meowed in spite of himself, as joy coursed through him. Momma followed him, carefully guiding him away from any possible danger. He delighted in the wind ruffling through his fur, the tantalizing scents of coming Leaf Bloom on the air. Phantom appeared from behind the house.

"Look! Momma let me come out!" Khan called to his best friend.

Phantom hurried to his side.

"I am so happy you feel strong enough to enjoy this." Phantom touched noses with him, tail straight up behind him.

"I am very weak," Khan admitted. "But this is so invigorating."

"Khan? Is that you? Where have you been?" The familiar voice turned Khan's head. Black strode up the lawn, but, as he drew closer, his pace slowed. His eyes widened with shock.

"Oh, my, you are so thin." Black stopped, stretched his neck, and briefly touched noses with Khan. "Your scent is alarming. Oh, no. Oh, no."

"Black?"

"I am sorry, old friend, I am so sorry."

"About what?" Khan sat down, fear racing through him.

"The sickness has you. It will kill you. It will hurt so."

"Black," Phantom snarled. "That is enough!"

"I am so sorry, so sorry," Black whimpered. "But I am sure you both know the truth."

"I do. Please don't be sorry," Khan mewled. "I want to be happy this day."

"Then enjoy the sun. Be happy." Black stood up, and a tremor went through him. "You fought the good fight, and that is all any of us can do. I will miss you."

Black whirled, and ran down the lawn, uttering a wail of grief. Khan trembled.

"Miss me?"

"Ignore him."

"I can't. You said it, too. That I smell very wrong. Black is very smart."

"I know. Try not to think about it. Just enjoy the day." Phantom urged. "The sun is so warm. The grass smells so good, and the soil is alive with motion and wonderful scents. Explore with me." Khan stared at him a moment, then turned his attention to the wonders of the outdoors. He forgot Black's words, as the excitement of the foray sent strength into his thin legs. He drank in the sweet grass, chewed on the tender blades, inhaled the scent of greening bushes, and pawed the warm soil. When he shook with exhaustion, Momma brought him back inside.

"No, Momma! I want to stay outside," he protested, but let Momma carry him in as fatigue overwhelmed him. As he navigated the floors, his feet slipped, and he wobbled unsteadily. Pain shot through his middle, brief but sharp. He uttered a growling cry, unable to stifle it. Momma watched him, worry on her face.

"You OK, sweet one? You don't hurt, do you?"

Khan walked to her, and purred. She gazed down at him, and he knew his purr fooled her no longer. He turned, and went to the food dishes and ate, hoping to change the expression on her face and the emotions radiating from her entire being.

That evening, he slowly ambled into the livingroom, and, gathering himself, leaped for Momma's chair. His claws latched onto the blanket, and his midsection struck the soft-cushioned end of the recliner. He lost his grip, then fell to the rug. He shook himself as Poppy exclaimed, "He fell!"

"Oh, no!" Momma cried, sitting up. She scooped him up, cradling him to her chest, and lay him gently on the cover. "Are you OK, honey bear?"

Khan purred rough, ashamed that he failed his leap, fearing his growing weakness. He settled in Momma's embrace, purring to throttle the cries of pain that tried to burst from his throat.

Later, in his bedcage, he huddled on the soft bedding. Pain wracked his insides, and he purred, trying to comfort himself.

"You're real sick now. You're getting sicker so fast," Phantom said softly, sitting beside the cage. Warlocke joined him.

"I am scared," Warlocke mewled. Indy sat under the table, eyes wide, tail wrapped tight to his body.

"I am, too," Khan meowed softly, and curled up. He slept fitfully, waking many times as pain lanced through his body. When early dawn light filtered through the windows, Khan woke for good. He huddled, feeling weary and cold. Shortly after sunrise, Momma came downstairs. She opened his cage, and Khan looked up at her, purred loudly, but refused to move.

"What is the matter, baby?" Momma gently grasped him, and pulled him out. He lay on the floor, purring, gazing up at her, lacking the energy to put his legs in motion. Momma picked him up, forcing him to move. His legs buckled, and he fell. She lifted him again, tears in her eyes, and he tottered over to the water dish, drank, then made his way to the livingroom, falling over twice on the hard slate of the foyer. He uttered one cry of pain, entered the livingroom, then huddled on the rug in misery.

"I scent much badness," Phantom said softly, looking down from Momma's chair. Khan gazed at his friend in silence, feeling pain lance through him as his body shut down little by little. He heard Momma talking on the phone, her voice shaking with grief. Suddenly, she came into the livingroom, gently lifted him, and brought him to the familiar cat carrier. Her sobs filled Khan's ears. Phantom let out a wail, and bolted upstairs. Warlocke and Indy scattered in fear.

"Noooooo!"

Khan uttered mews of fear as Momma drove him to the Animal Hospital. She talked to Khan, but he barely heard her as pain overcame his fears. At the cat doctor, Khan waited, his energy rapidly fading. He found no fears -- only pain and weariness. A strange cold sensation enveloped him, and it reached deep into his very bones. It felt colder than the most frigid winter wind, but, oddly, he did not shiver as his energy reserves dried up. In the exam room, he did not protest when the doctor took him out of the box. The cat nurse picked him up, and pain shot through his stomach. He wailed in anguish, causing Momma to call to him.

"Baby, what's wrong? Why are you crying?"

Khan only meowed, eyes wide, as the nurse returned him to the table.

"Only eight point five pounds."

"Oh, no," Momma gasped. "He's lost almost a full pound in five days. He should be seventeen pounds. He's not getting anything out of his food. The cancer is eating it all."

"I know," the doctor said quietly. "I can feel the one kidney. It's swollen so much it reaches clear across his body. The other I can't find -- oh, here it is. It, too, is very enlarged. The lymphoma is winning."

"It is, no matter what we do," Momma wept. Khan lay still, looking at the doctor and his momma through bleary vision. He felt numb, and the shock of pain drained the last of his fears and energy. Momma spoke with the doctor, and sobbed openly now.

"Temp is only 98.6," the doctor murmured. "He hasn't the energy to fight any longer. He's dying."

"He just started crying out loud yesterday," Momma said. "I can't stand to know he's in pain."

"I know it's a difficult decision," the doctor said softly, "but it is the kindest. He will only feel more and more pain."

"I know," Momma inhaled a big sob. "Let's do it."

"You must be ready," the doctor said.

"I will never be ready to let him go, never, but it's the right thing to do."

Khan flicked his ear. Let go? Let go of what? Momma stroked him, and her tears fell on his head. He blinked, unable to purr to her. The doctor returned, and stuck a needle in his hip. He barely felt it. Crying hard now, Momma picked him up, wrapping him in the soft towel he always laid upon in the carrier. She sat down, hugging him to her chest, and rocked him. The pain ebbed, and he felt sleepy. His muscles relaxed, and he tried to purr, comforted by Momma's embrace. She rocked him, talking to him, but he heard only the love and grief in her tones. His vision faded to grey, and he fell into a wonderful painless slumber, hearing Momma's voice, inhaling Momma's scent, feeling her touch. All went black.

Suddenly, awareness returned to Khan, and he found himself standing on top of his own body. He saw the exam room with crystal clarity, saw Momma bending down over the table, crying. In surprise, he looked down at his own face. He uttered a strong purr as quick realization struck him.

"Black, Mandee was right! You *can* see and scent after the Big Sleep! This is the Big Sleep!"

He drifted upward, and, above him, The Rift he feared for so long appeared in the very fabric of the air. The room around him greyed as The Rift exerted a pull on him. He peered into it, and saw a peaceful place, where every being drifted through blue and white mists as if asleep, eyes closed, bodies prone. He noticed with sudden alarm that all of them -- cat, dog, human, horse, and wild animals alike -- floated like wraiths -- transparent entities which drifted toward a Vortex of swirling colors. He glanced down again, realizing he floated above his body. The Rift pulled at him with a steady relentless force. He suddenly knew with clear understanding his predicament. Memories of Mandee's ascent into such a vortex flooded his mind.

"Nooooo!" he wailed at The Rift. "Nooooo! I won't leave my momma! NO! I won't be reborn! I don't want a new life and a new momma! I want THIS one! Noooo!"

He pulled energies from his grieving momma, channeling all the love he ever felt in his life into his efforts to resist The Rift. Khan extended his four legs with a new strength, and latched every nail into the towel under his body. His claws flared solid briefly, as they locked with the fabric of the towel. The room returned clearly to his senses, and, as The Rift pulled, he keened, refusing to let go. He barely noticed when the vet tech arrived to take his body away. The Rift swirled, as if confused, swinging between him and the direction his body went. Khan held tight to the towel. Momma's hands passed through his legs as she folded it. He shifted his grip in response, moving his paws swiftly. She put the towel in the carrier, and the room blurred before his eyes. He screamed denials, feeling the fabric slip in his claws, until the familiar cat carrier materialized around him. His claws continued to glimmer between solid and transparent, keeping him firmly anchored to his familiar towel. He peeked out at The Vortex and hissed, clutching the terry cloth in all four transparent feet.

"Go away! I'm not going!"

To his surprise and relief, The Rift closed and vanished, whisking away after the cat nurse who handled his body. As Momma carried the crate out into the reception area, Khan caught sight of Oliver snoozing on the desk in a cozy cat bed.

"Oliver!" he called.

Oliver jerked awake. Khan waved a translucent paw thru the bars. "I did it! I'm a spirit, like Mandee was. I'm going home with my momma!"

"Khan! I am happy for you!" Oliver called, his voice full of astonishment, as Khan and his Momma went out the door. "But beware! The Vortex will come! I don't know how you can fight it again."

"I will, somehow! Thank you, friend!" Khan cried, as the door shut behind him. Momma opened the car door, and placed the carrier on the seat. She sat beside it, and started the car, crying. The car surged onto the main road. Khan looked out at her.

"Momma, Momma, don't cry! I am here!" He tried to utter his bobcat meow, and, to his dismay, only he heard it. He flicked his tail, fascinated as it sliced through the carrier wall with no ill effects. With a touch of sadness, he understood Momma would never see him again. He vowed to somehow make her know he still stood at her side, strong and pain-free, healed. As the car carried him and his momma along, Khan purred, then reached out and placed a paw on Momma's leg. His claws passed harmlessly through her thigh, but he steadied his paw so it rested on her jeans.

"Don't cry. Don't be sad. I'll be with you always, Momma."

# CHAPTER 24: THE RIFT

Khan clung to the carrier as Momma swung it from the car. He glimpsed familiar sights while Momma walked across the driveway, down the lawn, and into the house. She placed the carrier on the floor, crying with grief. Khan released the towel he clung to, and slipped past the closed door with ease. He glanced back at the bars, amazed he felt nothing while passing through them.

"Momma! Don't cry! I'm here."

He tried rubbing against her legs, but fell over, his body passing through her legs like a paw through air. He huddled on her feet, but her feet moved through his body. He stood up, shook himself, then sat under the dining room table, befuddled. He watched Momma dismantle his bedcage, and sadness engulfed him. Momma wept, and Khan wanted to comfort her, show her he still stayed by her side.

"Momma, I'm here, I really am," he called to her when she folded up the bedcage and took it upstairs. Momma returned, and swept the floor. After she finished that task, she opened the front door. To Khan's delight, Phantom sauntered into the hallway, tail raised.

"Phantom?"

"Khan?" Phantom meowed with surprise, and rushed into the dining room. He stopped, shock and delight rippling the hair on his body. "It is you! I thought you went to the Big Sleep."

"I did. You can see me?"

"Yes!" Phantom walked up to Khan, and delicately touched noses. Phantom's sea-green eyes widened. "You are like Mandee was! How did you get here? Is there a tin in the other room?"

"No tin." Khan answered. "I refused to let The Vortex take me, and held very tight to my towel. I rode home in the carrier."

"But Mandee said she stayed with her body. You didn't?"

"No."

"Khan! You're back!" Warlocke trotted into the room, tail aloft with joy. He halted, his tail drooping, eyes widening. "I can see through you! Why?"

"I escaped The Vortex when I went to the Big Sleep."

"Like Mandee did," Warlocke said, then flattened his ears. "Did you come back in a tin? You just left this morning."

"I stayed with the carrier. I did not want to leave Momma, even for a moment."

A short hiss silenced the conversation. Indy stood in the doorway, fur bristling, eyes wide.

"What happened to you? I can see through you!" Indy yowled.

"I went to the Big Sleep. But I refused to let The Vortex take me."

"I didn't see a new tin inside! How can this be?"

"I stayed with Momma, not my body," Khan explained patiently. "I was able to tap into our bond, and used it to hook my claws into the towel." Khan fixed his gaze on Indy, remembering what Mandee did to him when she defied The Vortex. "I think it is time for some real fun!"

Khan bounded toward Indy. Stars flared from his body, trailing from the tip of his long bushy tail. Indy stood his ground.

"She couldn't hurt me. You can't either."

"Don't be so sure," Khan answered with a rumbling growl. Khan slapped Indy's head, using his inner strength and power to solidify his paw. Indy jumped back, hissing in shock.

"Yeeeooooooww! That hurt!"

Khan swiped again, this time connecting with Indy's shoulder. Tiny stars exploded from the impact site, as Khan mastered control of his power. Indy hissed, then whirled away, racing for the stairs. Khan followed, smacking Indy's rump. The tabby-and-white Maine Coon darted back down the stairs, up the hall, and into the kitchen. Khan raced on Indy's tail, thoroughly enjoying himself. Indy fled from him, eyes wide, tail tucked, body low, and dashed past Momma while she worked on the computer. After his third pass, Momma gazed at Indy, her brow raised.

"Indy, what is wrong with you today? There is nothing there."

"Yes, there is." Indy glanced up at Momma, but his soft answer went unheard.

"She can't see me," Khan responded. "She thinks you've gone crazy."

Indy raced upstairs. Khan followed gleefully while Phantom and Warlocke watched from under the table. Again, Indy ran through the house back to the kitchen, Khan merrily slapping his tucked tail.

"He's so scared he can't even hiss," Phantom commented.

"Unlike Mandee's, my slaps hurt," Khan laughed in response. All afternoon and into the night, he chased Indy around the house, letting up only to allow Indy to eat, use the litterbox, and take a breather. Finally, in the hours before dawn, Indy sagged to the rug in the upstairs hallway.

"Please," he begged. "Stop! I'm so sorry I bothered you when you were sick."

"You're sorry?" Khan sat down. "You never said that to Mandee."

"She never really hurt me. Your strikes sting." Indy flattened his ears, pulling back his whiskers. "Please, I'm tired."

"OK, I'll stop. I just hope you've learned a lesson."

Indy remained silent, and laid down on the brown rug. Khan left him, and trotted downstairs, meeting Phantom in the kitchen.

"Are you going to eat?" Phantom asked.

"I don't need to eat or use the potty box," Khan answered, sitting down beside his buddy.

"Not need to eat? I can't imagine that," Phantom commented around a mouthful of kibble.

Khan watched, amused, happy to be home again.

The sky outside lightened, and, soon, Momma and Poppy came downstairs, going about the normal daily routines of life. Momma sat at the table with Poppy, sipping coffee. A sudden meow turned Khan's attention away from his beloved humans. Silhouetted in the kitchen window sat a very familiar figure.

"Black!" Khan exclaimed, recognizing his old friend. He easily leaped onto the sink, then glanced in alarm at Momma, until he remembered that she no longer saw him. She only responded to Black's meows, and put his breakfast on the back porch. Khan's unease vanished, and he pushed his nose against the screen.

"Khan? Is that you?" Black's meows sharpened with shocked surprise. "You look great! What . . ." Black trailed off before continuing. "I can see through you."

"I went to the Big Sleep. The sickness took me," Khan explained, walking through the screening. He sat in front of Black on the roofing.

"How are you here?" Black bristled with insight. "You are a spirit! The Vortex did not take you?"

"It tried. It couldn't take me because I wanted to stay with my momma."

"But you and Phantom both said it came for Mandee, and she could not stay. Why is this different? Won't it come for you again?"

"It might." Khan flattened his ears briefly. "I will fight it if it does."

"Mandee tried to fight it. She failed in the end," Black argued softly.

"I refuse to leave my momma! I don't want to be born into a new kitten, and get another Momma!" Khan hissed in sudden fury and denial.

"You defy Natural Law." Black sat still, enduring the stars and sparks that showered his body.

"I refuse to leave," Khan growled.

"The Vortex is real, Khan. It will come for you," Black mewled, his eyes wide and sad. "It cannot be denied."

"I will fight it every time I see it," Khan retorted. Khan reached out, and, using what he learned, manipulated the power he possessed, touching Black with a solid paw. "I am stronger than Mandee was. I can do things she couldn't, like come out here to sit with you, and I spanked Indy. He said my swats hurt."

"It may give you more time, but it will win eventually. But, until it does, visit me often."

"I will," Khan agreed.

To Khan's delight, a mooncycle passed, and The Vortex never materialized. Khan enjoyed dawn visits with Black, going for long jaunts around the old black cat's territory, and even followed Black into his old home once, when his Poppy allowed it. Black's housemate Oscar, a pretty shaded silver-and-white part-Maine Coon who resembled Indy, dashed away from Khan in terror.

"Because of conflict with Oscar, " Black explained, " I stay outdoors nowadays. Your Momma feeds me, too. She watches out for me."

"That makes me happy. I worried about you after he moved in."

Khan purred, enjoying the time he spent with his old friend. Phantom often joined him and Black during the day. Khan enjoyed racing through the yards with his friends, something he always longed to do in life. He learned that what Phantom told him suncycles ago held truth. Too many times his spirit-self fell from trees, or ran into the path of an oncoming car. Momma protected him all his life from himself.

Khan cuddled with Momma at night, snuggling beside Phantom on her lap, wishing she knew he still was with her. He passed through the bedroom door, and slept on the bed beside Momma every night, content to be in her presence. He accepted that she never knew he remained with her, but wished so very much to comfort her when she grieved for him.

During the following mooncycle, Momma brought his tin home. She cried, and Khan followed her, trying to will himself to her sight. For a full mooncycle, he struggled in vain to let her know of his presence. One night, he relaxed beside Phantom on Momma's recliner.

"You seem tired," Phantom commented.

"I am. I can't get Momma to see me. I hate to see her cry."

"We all do," Phantom said softly. "Are you going upstairs to sleep?"

"I tried already. I couldn't get through the door." Khan gazed at his lifelong friend. "I am losing power."

"You expend too much energy trying to solidify to the point where she can see you. You can't."

Suddenly, the air just below the ceiling fan crackled. Bright sparks shot down into the dark room, as a jagged blue slash appeared, floating down toward Khan.

"No!" Khan reared up, stars and sparkles exploding from his body. Phantom hissed, leaping from the chair. Khan sank his claws into the recliner, trying to solidify his claws. They flickered bright once, before he lost his strength. The Vortex descended, its blue maw widening. Khan shut his eyes and wailed his despair. Some force snatched him by the nape of his neck, shook him gently, and hauled him free of the chair. He opened his eyes, watching the room he loved drop from under his feet.

"Noooooooooooo!" he howled in misery. "Noooo! Mommmmmmmmaaaaaaaa!"

The Vortex sucked him in, veiling Khan's vision. His best friend's terrified grief-stricken face stared at him through the closing fog.

"Nooo! Pleeeaaase!" Khan wailed into the swirling icy-blue mists. Despite his anguish, his eyelids sagged, and his memories faded with each passing moment. He clung to the thought of Phantom and Momma, fighting the impulse to relax and sink into darkness. His energies failed, but he used the very last dregs to utter one howl of determination before the blackness engulfed him.

"Mommmmmmmaaaaaa! I'll never leave you! I will come home!"

## CHAPTER 25: RED MAGIC KITTEN

Suckling warm milk from his mother's breast, the tiny newborn kitten came slowly to awareness. His mother's scent engulfed his nostrils, as he filled his stomach with nourishment. He floated in serene darkness, until, one day, his tiny ears perceived sound. Not long after, his eyes opened, revealing a wondrous world to his young mind. He yearned to explore, filled with a deep need he did not understand.

He worried little over the feelings, as the days flowed into one another, and he wrestled his six siblings, growing fast and strong. His mother uttered a loud twittery call each time she returned to the kittening box. He always led the charge to her side, and she comforted him with her deep rumbling purrs.

One warm dawn, his mama's human momma and poppy gathered him, his mama, and his siblings, and placed them in strange boxes. To his horror, the boxes moved. He mewled in fear.

"Do not fret, Little Red," his mama purred, licking his head. "We are leaving our vacation place in Maine, and going home."

"Going home?" Little Red forgot his fear at those words. A faint stab of longing reached deep into him. "Good place?"

"Yes, my little one, a good place. All of us are going home, to a place called upstate New York. See? Your daddy, my human momma and poppy, and all the other cats who live with us are here on this journey."

Mollified, Little Red snuggled against his mother. The journey ended before sunset. Little Red gazed wide-eyed as the humans carried him and his family to their new living quarters. The bright room bathed in sunlight filled Little Red with energy. He and his littermates explored the place. Over the next several days, their mother taught them to eat solid food, and to use the proper box for toilet duties.

One morning, strange human footsteps echoed from downstairs. His mama's human walked into his bright domain, followed by strangers. He and his siblings endured handling by this couple, who laughed and talked loudly. Another couple who had human kittens came later. The young humans squealed, and grabbed at him and his littermates. Little Red played with the humans, but the boisterous noise and commotion scared two of his sisters into hiding. Once the visitors left, the two little girls peeked out from under the dresser.

"Can come out?" asked Little Red's smaller red sister.

"Yes, Tiny Red," Razzleberry, their mama, trilled to both sisters. "You, too, Pretty One."

Both female kittens poked their heads out, gazing at Little Red and their mother with wide blue eyes.

"Why you scared?" Little Red asked.

"Too much noise," Pretty One answered, and squeezed her little tortoiseshell body out from under the dresser. Tiny Red followed her.

"You scardy-kittens," Little Red's larger tortoiseshell sister said, and boldly leaped on Little Red.

"Little Razzie!" Little Red mewled, and wrestled back. His red tabby brother joined the tussle. In moments, the entire litter forgot the frightening visitors, and romped in glee all over their sunny realm.

The next morning, while Little Red and his siblings napped after a boisterous play session, strange human footfalls echoed in the house again. In terror, Tiny Red and Pretty One dove under the dresser. Little Red lay on the cat bed with his brown tabby brother, and their larger red tabby brother. Little Red's dark brown tabby brother lay on the floor by the food bowl, snoozing. Little Razzie romped around the room.

"Aren't you tired?" Little Red yawned.

"No. Play time!" Little Razzie ran out into the hall, despite the strange footfalls which grew louder.

"Oh, how cute!" A strange human's voice floated up into the room. "Little bibis -- oh, they are sooo cute!"

Little Red twitched his ears, and listened. The voice sent a thrill through his body, as the strange visitor entered the room. Beside him, sprawled on the floor, Big Red slept, unaware of the invasion. His brown tabby brother, Big Boy, twitched his ears and yawned. On the floor by the food dish, Shadow slept, oblivious to everything. The stranger sat, and placed her belongings on the bed. Little Red eyed those items with sudden interest, and jumped up on the bed to investigate. The scents invading his small nose intrigued him, and he felt flashes of familiarity that made no sense. The stranger handled his littermates, then picked him up from the bed. Little Red wiggled in protest, and when the stranger laid him in her arms, he nibbled on her skin.

"No bites!" she laughed at him. He stopped biting, and licked her arm, then gazed up at her face. He relaxed, and purred, inexplicably drawn to the stranger. He mouthed her fingers, then licked them, and the scent entering his nostrils seemed so familiar, yet he knew this strange human never came to visit him and his siblings before this day. Confusion clouded his mind, and he wiggled, wanting to get down. The visitor placed him back on the bed, where he dashed for the intriguing articles there. The hauntingly familiar scents clinging to the items drew him like a moth to light.

"Fun stuff!" he called to his littermates. They ignored him, as his mama walked in, trilling to her kittens. He ran to the edge of the bed, but did not join his siblings. He looked back at the interesting pile of things.

"Come on! Fun stuff!" he called out.

"Now, Little Red, don't damage the visitor's belongings," his mama warned.

"Won't!" Little Red twittered a reply, and ran across the bed, ready to turn and pounce on his new-found toys. He suddenly found himself face to face with the visitor. Emotion fired through him, driving him to drop his head and roll, until he gazed at her upside down. She smiled at him, and a spark of affection startled him. He jumped up, ran back to the visitor's belongings, and scratched on the papers.

"Little Red!"

"Not hurting them," Little Red retorted. "Fun!"

He wrestled with the items, ignoring the bright flashes of light from a camera in the room, until the visitor picked up the items. He sat on the bed, watching, as the stranger left the room. As her footfalls faded, Little Red felt inexplicable upset.

"Why she leave? Why take toys away?" he asked, jumping down to his mama's side.

"Those were her possessions, not yours," Razzleberry explained.

"Oh." Little Red sat down.

"Those things belonged to her. She didn't bring them here for you."

"They seemed like mine," Little Red argued. "Why did she leave?"

"All visitors leave, sweet red one," Razzleberry said.

"I want her to come back and play with me, and being back the toys!"

"She will come back," Razzleberry assured him. "Most visitors come back."

"She will?"

"Yes, sweetie, all of you will go to new homes, and get new human mommas. One of these visitors may be your new human momma."

At Razzleberry's last words, a stab of fear drilled deep into Little Red. He understood none of it, but his response erupted unbidden, driven by a whirlwind of strange images and feelings.

"I don't want a NEW human momma! Never ever want NEW human momma!!!!"

"Little Red!" Razzleberry gaped at him in shock. "You know you can't stay here with me forever."

"I know, Mama, but I so scared! Feel like so sad, scared. Don't want new human momma, but don't know why." Little Red mewled, snuggling up to his mother. "I see and feel strange things in my mind. Feel things. And when you say new momma, I not want! Nooo!"

"Shush, my sweet little boy," Razzleberry purred, and licked his head. "Think a moment. Did all the visitors scare you? Did not one seem like you might want her as a new momma?"

"I like last one, but too scared." Little Red trembled. "She make me see strange things and feel things. I'm scared."

"I know you are, but you may be experiencing something very, very special."

"What?" Little Red peered up at Razzleberry's tortoiseshell face.

"Well, after a cat's life is over, and we go to the Big Sleep . . ."

"BIG SLEEP?" Little Red cried out, terror racing his heart. "NOOO!"

"How can you know what that is?" Razzleberry stared down at him, green eyes widening.

"Place of darkness!" Little Red yowled.

"Yes, it is," Razzleberry continued, and Little Red heard the suppressed shock in his mother's purr. "But how you know of it is a mystery. You're so young. You have no need to fear the Big Sleep."

"Why?" Little Red trembled, but faced his mother bravely.

"You're healthy and strong. Only very sick or very old cats go to the Big Sleep. But let me explain a wondrous thing to you. Try not to be afraid, Little Red."

"OK, Mama."

"Now, once a cat passes from this world, the life energies are reborn into another cat, when they are made inside a mama cat."

"How?" The question echoed from on the bed, where all Little Red's siblings gathered, eyes wide with wonder.

"All life is energy, and when our bodies fail, that energy is taken, and, through a portal of sorts, is absorbed by a new life, and becomes a new kitten." Razzleberry cocked her head. "We never remember who we once were or what other human mommas or poppas we may have had. When new babies are created in me, like all of you were, the energies are drawn to them, and thus new life grows and prospers."

"Why don't we know our before-times then?" asked Little Razzie.

"Because it is just energy that is part of the world. We may receive this energy, but we are our own selves. Most of what we are is in our genes. The energy is just force that finds us, and gives us growth and life." Razzleberry dropped her gaze to Little Red. "However, sometimes the bond between a cat and human momma is so very strong that something in the energy is changed. Sometimes energy patterns of old memories and feeling are captured, and travel to the next life. It is very rare. I think, Little Red, you may be experiencing this gift of the cat spirits."

"Me? Why?"

"You said you saw and felt strange things. You may be getting flashes of memory and emotion from your energies. Why, I cannot say. Nobody knows for sure, though I met one female at a show who insisted she was reborn and reunited with her beloved human momma. Said she remembered everything. There is no way to prove it for sure, but why would she lie?"

"I'm scared," Little Red mewled. "If I have those things but don't ever get my momma back, what will happen?"

"Nothing bad, little one. In time, the disturbing feelings may go away. If this has happened to you, you can only wait, and try not to fear." Razzleberry licked his head.

Little Red tried to understand all the spiritual concepts in his six-week-old mind. He comprehended little, and felt only confusion. He slowly relaxed under his mother's brisk tongue wash, and, soon, fell asleep.

When Little Red awoke the next morning, all the conversation and worry seemed a distant dream. He romped with his siblings in the warm room. Days merged into each other as visitors came and went, and his fears diminished. The weird sensations of that day did not return.

By the beginning of Leaf Fall, Little Red forgot the entire incident. One cool sunny morning, his mother's human momma came upstairs, scooped him up, and hurried back downstairs. Little Red perked up, eyeing parts of the house previously shut off to him. His mama's human deposited him on a low table, but before he lifted a paw to go explore, hands grasped him. They scooped him into an embrace, and a weird feeling of familiarity shot through him. He inhaled, and recognized the scent belonging to the visitor he liked from a mooncycle ago. The visitor hugged him, and Little Red sensed some deep distress from her. It unsettled him, and he wiggled in her grip. The stranger lowered him into a plastic box with cage bars for a lid. Fear raced through Little Red.

"Mama! Mama!" he cried. But nobody answered. He suddenly recalled the conversation of a mooncycle ago.

"No! I don't want a new human momma! Want my momma!"

He wailed, without understanding what he felt. The stranger lifted the box, and carried him out of the house. He sensed her emotional state, and yowled, fear rising to rule his mind and emotions.

"Oh, little Kai, don't make Momma cry, too," the stranger said in a quavering voice, as she belted him into a huge metal box with wheels. He vaguely recalled such things, from early kittenhood, when his family moved from one home to another. He pawed at the bars, rolling on his back, disliking the confined space. He looked at the stranger, and knew she was his new momma, whether he wanted it or not. She sat next to him, and the big box rumbled to life. Kai wailed with new fright. Odd memories and feelings pummeled his heart and mind.

"Kai, don't cry, sweetie," his new momma said. "We'll be home soon."

Little Red mewled, and watched his momma, deciding he liked his new name. Something seemed comforting about it. The motion of the box startled him, and he clawed at the bars, trying to free himself.

"Kai, please, don't be so scared," Momma said, her voice shaking. She placed her hand on the bars, and Kai relaxed as her scent filled his nose. Despite his fears, he knew he traveled with the right momma. She cried, and her sadness sliced into his own fears.

"Don't cry so much, Kai. I know it's a long ride, but we'll be home soon." Momma said.

Kai tried to quell his dread, but the rumble of traffic and Momma's nervousness kept him on edge during the long journey. He rolled around in the carrier, pulling at the metal bars, crying out his desperation. Only when she placed a hand on the bars, and Kai smelled her scent, did he feel any comfort.

"Momma, why cry? Why sad? Why? I'm scared!"

"You seem to get upset when I pull my hand away. Sweetie, I need it to drive. Try to relax. We are almost home," Momma said, then her voice dropped. Water leaked from her eyes. "Oh, Khan, my sweet teddy bear, how I miss you so. You'd love this sweet little one."

The name Khan struck a chord deep within Kai. He stopped mewling, and watched his new momma intently. Vague memories flashed through his mind, and, suddenly, he knew he belonged with this momma, his momma. He took the time to study his surroundings, and, in an instant, the vehicle around his carrier looked hauntingly familiar. The car came to a stop, and Momma lifted his crate out, carrying it across a driveway and lawn. Kai peered out of the bars, sniffing deeply. The scents, sounds, and sights enveloped him with security. She brought him into the house, lowered his carrier to the floor, and opened the top. Kai sat up, peering out, just as three adult cats converged on the room. Fearing entrapment, Kai leaped from the box, arched his back in an instinctive response, and hissed. The largest cat, a huge dark-silver tabby with short hair, approached.

"Behave, mere kitten. I rule here."

"Don't hurt me!" Kai hissed back, even as his senses reeled with deep recognition. "Know you!"

"How?" The huge cat stared at him, his sea-green eyes wide.

Kai glanced at the other two long-haired cats, and he recognized both of them on a deep level he did not comprehend yet. "Know you, too!"

"No! It can't be!" the tabby-and-white longhair yowled, disbelief in his eyes. "It can't be him!"

"What if it is, Indy?" The other cat, a black longhair with silvery ruff, britches, and belly shag, replied with mirth. "You'd best watch your butt."

"Shut up, Warlocke! It's not him anyway! Can't be!" Indy hissed, and bolted from the room. The cat Indy called Warlocke slanted his ears back, and hissed, but he regarded Kai with gentle green eyes.

"Know you, too, in a weird way. But you still new." The black longhair sat down. "All kittens must learn house rules."

"How do you know him, Warlocke? How?" The shorthaired cat hissed, but sniffed Kai's back. "Scent not same. Not true."

"Next time you see Black, ask him," Warlocke retorted. "He will know."

"Black?" Kai asked, forgetting his kitten status. "Know that name! Know!"

"How?" the shorthair asked with a hiss. "You are but a kitten, and a newcomer. You've never been here before."

"Yes, here," Kai insisted, looking around the room, knowing deep down that he finally arrived where he belonged. "My mama right. I special. I return to my momma!"

The shorthair stared aghast. Kai sidled up to the huge cat.

"Know you! Me Kai! What your name? I guess Fan? Fanom?"

"Close guess, but it is Phantom," the big shorthair growled, eyes wide with surprise.

"Yes! Know! Phan-tom!" Kai's excitement rose. He felt no more fear of any of the felines. "Want to play now?"

"Can't be," Phantom growled. "You are not Khan!"

"Not Khan. I'm Kai! But," Kai replied, flicking his long tail as he thought out his words, "Khan born in me. This Khan's home, so is mine."

"Can't be!" Phantom hissed, and ran from the room. Kai sensed Phantom's anguish. Feelings for the huge shorthair filled Kai's heart. He faced the silvery-black longhair.

"I show him this true. I will."

"You will, in time," Warlocke agreed, then hissed suddenly in warning. "But you are still new here. You can't just take his spot, and think you are him."

"I not him, but . . . am him," Kai mewled, feeling unexplained hurt. Warlocke turned, and walked from the room, leaving Kai alone with Momma. He gazed around the room, which blanketed him with old familiar security. All his fear and anxiety drained away, and he spotted the toy box under the hutch. Jubilation flashed through him, driving away the last of his uncertainty. He ran to the basket, and gleefully pulled out jiggle balls, sponge balls, furry mice, and catnip toys. Their scent filled his nostrils, sparking vague memories which grew stronger, solidifying in his mind. As he explored the house, he puffed with inner pride, knowing what lay ahead of his questing senses. He glanced backward at Phantom and Warlocke, who followed his forays.

"See? Know what past that door." Kai sat on a brown rug in front of a closed door.

"What, smart butt?" Phantom growled, but, in his tone, Kai heard acceptance.

"Momma's room. She and Poppy sleep there. Fun place." Kai ran to the louvered door at the end of the hall. "Ohhhhh! Fun, fun! At-tic!"

"He does know," Warlocke said quietly. "We can't deny something wonderful happened."

"I still can't believe it," Phantom flattened his ears. "But I can't deny my own senses. If Demon is in me, then why not Khan in him?"

"Exactly," Warlocke purred. Kai faced both, and dashed past them to the steps.

"I hear you!" Kai paused at the top of the stairwell, and held Phantom's gaze. "I prove it to you. You see. Belong!"

He plunged down the steps, not waiting for a reply, and raced around the big house in sheer delight. He careened into the kitchen, until a loud very familiar meow halted him in his tracks. He looked up, and in the window over the sink, silhouetted by the setting sun, the face of a black cat peered at him. To the marrow of his little bones Kai knew that cat.

"Black! Black!"

"How do you know my name, Kid?"

"You old friend," Kai mewled, dancing in a circle under the window. "Now know Kai is home!

"Great good cat spirits! Khan! My old friend! You did it, didn't you?" Black gasped. "It's amazing. I have never seen such in all my years."

Kai stopped, and stared at the old cat. At his side, his new housemates stood, awe and wonder in their eyes. Kai met the black cat's gaze.

"I come home. Not Khan now. I am Kai," he announced proudly.

"Yes, yes, you are Kai. Worthy to walk Khan's pawprints. I see it in your eyes, old and new friend." Black pulled back, and left the rooftop. "I must go. Momma put out my dinner. Well-met, young Kai! Well-met!"

Kai stared at the open window for many minutes, emotions and dreamlike memories playing in his head.

"Good to see you, too," he mewled softly, then turned to Phantom. "You my friend, too."

"Yes, you are," Phantom nodded. "We will be best buddies, but," Phantom paused to bare the tips of his fangs, "you are still a little kitten who needs to learn the rules."

"Know rules," Kai retorted pompously, then gave Phantom a mischievous glance, before racing out of the room. "May make new ones!"

Later that evening, Momma picked him up, and cuddled him on her lap, while relaxing in a big soft chair. Joy infused his being, and he looked up into her face, purring loud and strong. She smiled.

"Silly kitten. You remind me so much of Khan," Momma said. "You soothe that ache in my soul, little one. Could you be my Khan reborn? Maybe such is possible, but no matter what, you fill my heart with love."

"Kai re-mem-ber. Remember!" he said, his mind filling with strange visions of blue mists. The next words inexplicably poured from his heart and mind. "I told you, Momma, I'm coming home! Kai now home!"

# EPILOQUE

Many mooncycls cycles passed. Kai grew into a powerful enormous twenty-four pound Maine Coon. The bond he sensed he shared with Phantom that first meeting suncycles ago, strengthened into the friendship and love of old, enduring for many seasons, until Phantom's passing at sixteen suncycles old shattered it asunder. To add injury to his broken heart, Black disappeared that following No Leaf season, and Momma grieved. Kai knew Black went to the Big Sleep, too.

Phantom (13 yeears old) & Kai (2 Years old-not yet fully grown)

After a long period of grieving, Kai recovered, and regained the weight he lost in the sad mooncycles. Momma started speaking of a new kitten arriving soon, and Kai waited with hope in his heart.

Little Orion, bought to the house by a human Momma called Niece, showed no fear and frolicked through the house in utter delight. The jet-black kitten with his shiny patent-leather coat gazed at Kai with round, knowing eyes from his little circular head. Momma called him Little Round Head, and in his mischivious eyes, Kai saw an very old familiar soul, and readily befriended Orion, but disappointment filled his heart.

Though the incredible bond he shared with Phantom never materialized, and Phantom's essence remained absent from his life, Kai healed in mind and body. He recovered the friendship he and Black once shared, but part of his heart remained empty and raw.

He turned to his Momma for what his anguished heart longed for, and received love, a shared sense of loss, and an extremely close bond with is momma. He missed Phantom, and as the mooncycles passed, he wondered why his best buddy never came home as Black obviously had, considering the strong bond Phantom shared, not only with their Momma, but with Kai himself.

Indy went to the Big Sleep not long after, shocking the household. Warlocke slept beside Indy the previous night in silent, sad, vigil, and the old Maine Coon missed his housemate more than he thought possible. Kai groomed Warlocke, trying to ease his grief, but knew Indy's bond to Momma and his elder housemate did not possess near enough strength to bring him home again.

The pain soon eased, and deep in his soul, Kai kept the questions locked away, knowing the Vortex acted not on wishes, but by the laws of nature.

Several mooncycles later, somewhere miles away, a tiny kitten was born. She suckled from her mama, until a commotion disrupted her solitude. Her mama's hiss reverberated in her tiny ears as something lifted her into the air, then dropped her into unfamiliar territory, filled with the scent of dogs. She heard barking, and shivered with cold, and mewling desperately for her Mama, who never responded. Suddenly, huge jaws closed over her, wet, drooling, but gentle, as a huge female Pitbull she later came to know as Smash, brought her to safety. Warmth enveloped her. The little kitten opened her eyes days later, already bonded to her Human Momma, who dubbed her Nala, feeling secure and happy as she suckled from her bottle, cuddled in her Momma's loving hands.

She remembered nothing of a former life, but one day, strange humans poked into her world, and their aromas filled her with deep attraction. She scented strange cats on this human her Momma called Aunt, and knew, even at her young age, she lived in her forever home, but something seemed missing.

Nala at 4 weeks old.

One day, mooncycles later, during Leaf Fall, her momma took her on a long journey to a strange place. Nala took the ride in stride, unafraid as long as her Momma stayed nearby. Momma and her family walked into an old house. Happy human voices surrounded Nala, and she scented the strange cats immediately, recognizing them from that day she caught whiffs of their odors on the strange humans many mooncycles ago.

Once on the floor, Nala surveyed the home, and everything seemed so familiar. She paraded through the house, feeling comfortable with everything that met her questing senses, feeling no fear, even when trailed by a very interested black smoke Maine Coon, who trilled to her, calling himself Warlocke. Turning into the kitchen, where the smell of food drew her, she came face to face with a huge male red tabby Maine Coon cat. She felt attraction, but did not approach him, her eyes widening at his enormous size.

He watched her, fascinated, from a chair under the table. She continued her roaming, eating food from the other cats' bowls. The enormous red cat stared at her, and when he spoke in his high-pitched voice, calling himself Kai, she sneezed feline mirth at such a high voice from so large a feline, but met his gaze. He called her by a strange name, and she held his eyes a long moment, before announcing her proper name to him. Nala admitted they intrigued her, and knew she found what she felt missing in her life.

She resumed her wandering, jumping up on the bathroom sink, drinking in everything. Warlocke followed her, excitement in his high voice as he called her by yet another name. The sense of familiarity filled her, and she considered perhaps these two knew something she possessed little understanding of. She told them her tale of abandonment and rescue by a huge, friendly, loving dog, who now obeyed her iron claws.

Kai blinked a feline chuckle, explaining to Nala why she strove to rule her canine family members. Nala sat, enthralled by the stories of Phantom's reign of his yard, and handling of aggressive dogs. Nala blinked a feline grin at tales of Indy's psychotic behaviors, and felt something stir in her heart. Could she be them?

At nightfall, her momma picked her up, and they left old house. Nala snuggled and fell asleep, feeling deep contentment, her dreams full of scents, sounds, and sights that told her subconscious mind the cats in the old house indeed knew something special occurred, but remembered little of these dreams once she returned home. She only knew she felt ties to that old house and its inhabitants.

Back in the house, Kai sniffed every corner the young female traversed, trailed by Warlocke who insisted he saw Indy within young Nala. Kai argued he saw Phantom in the juvenile female. Warlocke then remembered Phantom believed Demon lived within him, and remarked why not Phantom and Indy in Nala? Kai agreed, mystified, yet heartened by the possibility.

When he curled up with Momma that night, he wished Nala remained here with him, but he knew his best buddy might have found new life and a new home in the body of that young female. The thought healed an old dull aching void in his heart, but he hoped he'd see Nala again someday.